T0267678

RADICAL
EMPATHY

RADICAL EMPATHY

STORIES

ROBIN ROMM

FOUR WAY BOOKS

LIBRARY OF CONGRESS CATALOGING-IN-PUBLICATION DATA

Names: Romm, Robin, author.

Title: Radical empathy : stories / by Robin Romm.

Description: New York, New York : Four Way Books, 2024.

Identifiers: LCCN 2024000667 (print) | LCCN 2024000668 (ebook) | ISBN
   9781961897182 (trade paperback) | ISBN 9781961897199 (epub)

Subjects: LCSH: Short stories. | LCGFT: Short stories.

Classification: LCC PS3618.O654 R34 2024 (print) | LCC PS3618.O654
   (ebook) | DDC 813/.6--dc23/eng/20240311

LC record available at https://lccn.loc.gov/2024000667

LC ebook record available at https://lccn.loc.gov/2024000668

This book is manufactured in the United States of America and printed on acid-free paper.

Four Way Books is a not-for-profit literary press. We are grateful for the assistance
we receive from individual donors, public arts agencies, and private foundations
including the NEA, NEA Cares, Literary Arts Emergency Fund, and the
New York State Council on the Arts, a state agency.

We are a proud member of the Community of Literary Magazines and Presses.

For Don Waters

CONTENTS

Marital Problems

1

Do the Dead Grieve

21

Radical Empathy

39

The Flower

57

A Gun in the First Act

71

Beautiful Burn

89

The Healing Room

105

Soothsaying

123

Ars Parentis

139

What to Expect

153

MARITAL PROBLEMS

Victor and I crouch in the yard, trying to find where our five-year-old daughter, Lucy, has buried the bird. She made it a coffin—sweet, except that she made it out of my husband's father's binocular case. My husband didn't know his father, a birder—a deadbeat birder to be more precise. So, the binocular case came to him in a roundabout way a few months ago. Junk from the kitchen remodel litters our yard—an old sink, pieces of hacked-apart tile—a hazard, a disgrace, a child's wonderland. As we search, Victor piles the debris in the corner.

"That fucking guy," he says, trying to move a cast-iron sink basin.

We've been remodeling our kitchen for the better part of a year. That makes us sound fancier than we are. In truth, a guy's installing Ikea cabinets and tile we got at a seconds sale. New lights, new wiring. For this budget refresher, I interviewed seven men in Carhartts, many of them hazy-pupiled, a few of them so expensive I couldn't bear to relay the bids to Victor. I settled on Marco.

Victor would like to sue Marco for leaving us without a working kitchen for months on end. Victor would like to take a cosmic flyswatter and squish him against the wall. Cork him in a bottle and sink him to the bottom of the sea.

"I think Marco's having marital problems," I tell him, moving a rock and peering under it, testing to see if the earth's been disturbed.

"Whatever," my husband says. "He can still find some guys to move this shit." He has dirt on the top part of his shaggy sideburn. If he swipes at his brow again, he'll wipe it into his eye. I don't mention this to him. "His wife has nothing to do with this job." Victor takes a piece of wood and hurls it at the corner. "Anyway, what makes you say that?"

"I can just tell," I say.

Whenever I predict the dramas of other men, Victor frowns and squints. He doesn't care, really, if I know such things about my female friends. He'll often jump into the fray with that sort of gossip. He loves a good postpartum depression story, a colicky baby, and an eating disorder. But when I surmise a man's emasculating salary, his attraction to domineering women, his obvious lust for a clichéd paramour—a nanny, a personal trainer—Victor recoils. *You don't know that,* he'll say, and it becomes clear to me, the boy he was at sixteen.

"He wants to talk about it, but I never ask," I say.

Marco's hair curls around his forehead and his lips form surprisingly soft little pillows above a very perfect knob of a chin. He looks like Hansel all grown-up, a fairy-tale boy with his tool kit and leather belt and paint-spattered ladder. Except that he isn't happy, our Marco. He hasn't figured out how to throw the witch in the oven. Instead, he finds himself married to her.

This is, at any rate, my theory, assembled through tattered bits of small talk. His wife, a Brazilian woman named Rosie, wants kids. Marco mentioned this once while doctoring his coffee. But he doesn't want the complication. He has a daughter from another marriage, and that child was the reason for the divorce. Marco always talks to me—no matter the subject (hardware, contracts, his wife)—with a sultry little smirk.

I get the sense that Marco figures if he lingers in the kitchen long enough, I'll finally lose my inhibition. My obvious attraction to his compact body, those muscles that look carved from soap, will overwhelm me. I'll descend the stairs in a negligée, a look of raunchy hunger thickening my gaze. But I don't feel like telling this to my husband. It'll make him even more furious at the asshole hijacking our home. He'll ratchet up the rhetoric against Marco until we have no choice but to fire him. And who will complete this half-finished budget remodel in this expensive city if not Marco?

Lucy didn't actually bury the bird. Had she buried it, we could ask her where. Instead, while Victor and I attended an actual funeral for a colleague of mine who died of ovarian cancer at thirty-two, Lucy put the dead bird in its coffin and then lost interest in it. The babysitter, a woman we hired through a service, didn't want to leave a dead bird lying around, so she went ahead and buried it. The babysitter hasn't responded to my emails or calls, and so somewhere in the yard lies the bird. Or so Lucy told us. She's frequently entranced by the notion that truth is a malleable thing, so who knows what to believe.

Most of our yard is compact soil, nearly clay-like. Any disruption to it causes lumps and crumbs, which makes this bird burial particularly perplexing. We've tried places that appear to be stirred up, mostly near the fence or under vines, but so far, they've yielded nothing.

"He might just be depressed," my husband says. "Or hate being a contractor."

"Maybe," I say.

"Or maybe he doesn't like you."

"No, Marco likes me."

"I don't know why you think you know everything," my husband says. "Did he tell you that he has marital problems?"

"He definitely has marital problems. Think about it. When we ask him to do something, he sulks, he looks at the ground and acts like he hasn't heard. The kitchen job was an eight-week job. He's been here nine months, and it's not even done. When you follow up to see if a small task has been completed, he just stares. Can you imagine being his wife?"

"Yeah, that's true," my husband says. "What a dick that guy is."

"He's not a dick. He's just really passive. And slightly incompetent."

"Why do you defend him?" Victor asks.

"I'm not," I say.

"I should kick that guy's ass," my husband says. I try to imagine my husband taking down Marco. Victor used to have muscles like Popeye, bulbs sprouting seemingly off bone. But over the years he's become just plain skinny, with a small and polite little potbelly, a purse of flesh that Lucy likes to lie against while they read.

"Victor." I say his name sharply, like I'm snipping a thread.

The person Victor would really like to beat up, of course, is the deadbeat birder, but any man who comes around and tries to pull a fast one gets a tiny dose of Victor's ancient, private rage.

Several months ago, we got a call from a biological half-brother of Victor's who'd located Victor through a DNA testing service. Victor had sent off for results a few years prior, inspired by a longing for a clan after his mother died.

But he never did much with the information, so it surprised us when the half-brother, Quinn, emailed and asked if Victor wanted to meet. Yes, Victor did. Quinn detoured to Portland after a friend's wedding in Port Townsend. He showed up for dinner bearing flowers, a bottle of Syrah, their father's binoculars, and a dog-eared copy of *Birds of America*.

He worked as a paralegal for a big firm in San Jose. I thought he might be gay, though he never said as much. He exuded a tidiness, the kind that usually means that no woman washes your boxer shorts or puts away your laundry, enabling you to enjoy a lifetime of hetero-slovenliness; a tidiness that comes from doing all that bodily and sartorial maintenance yourself. He charmed us both. Lucy kept walking around his chair, gripping the back rung and shyly smiling, though Quinn didn't know what to do with a child and kept inching his chair closer to the table.

I can only tell you what's going on in the marriages of other people; I'm not sure what's going on in my own. It's Saturday, and our "morning alone time" has come to a close. We spent it all out here, looking for the binocular case. Maybe my marriage is like a beautiful weather vane on a regal barn, its edges soft, its tin turning turquoise and black. It used to spin beautifully, but the center's grown rusty. Maybe that's a dumb metaphor. That metaphor requires me to extend it, to say that these alone hours are the WD-40 we need. Maybe we're less weather vane and more tomato plant and this whole thing is fertilizer, or maybe we're just aging and sometimes I notice that my eyes are more revealed, the skin around them thin like that of a tomatillo. A hardness comes through places that used to be supple, and when Victor reaches for me in bed, it only feels like habit, the way we reach for our toothbrushes, and because I'm not a toothbrush, I turn away. I want to circumvent this fate, though I don't have the body for bustiers or the energy for finding politically acceptable, palatable, not completely obnoxious porn.

Last night, Lucy's friend Madeline slept over so that her mother, Danielle, could go on a date. Madeline had no idea that she'd been evacuated in order for her mother's house to become a den of seduction, but yesterday, when Danielle dropped off Madeline, she managed to show me her newly waxed legs.

Danielle was vague about the man, but I imagine he's some kind of artsy professional, an architect with a quick wit and intense libido. He stands in the kitchen—that gorgeous, airy kitchen—after a dinner of artichokes and oysters. Danielle's wavy red-blond hair is a little mussed, the strap of her slinky dress halfway down her arm. The bodice peels away slightly from her sternum, exposing a black lace bra. She steps out of her shoes, and he pulls down on the strap assuredly, until the breast reveals itself, a ripe peach in its netting, propped and framed. And he bites at it and she presses his head down toward her widening legs and he yanks the zipper of her dress, pulling it off like tissue paper to get to her underwear, also lace and easily removed. Then he hoists her up to that beautiful marble kitchen island, spreads her legs and goes at her like a ravenous teenager. Then when she's just about to come, he enters her, both of them groaning, wailing, convulsing as if being electrocuted—maybe the lights above them even go out, and semen spatters her fancy Scandinavian knife block.

In exchange for last night with Madeline, Danielle took Lucy this morning. Victor and I didn't crawl into bed together the second she left, though I still find him lovely, his black hair flecked with white and silver, his sharp jawline that could be used to trace right angles. Frequently, women at the grocery store chat him up. Once, a realtor closed the door to a bedroom of a house we were looking at buying—this was before Lucy, when I still worked my ruthless job at the domestic violence shelter and had to send Victor out to peruse new listings—and propositioned him. "What exactly did she say?" I wanted to know. Victor shrugged. "She said, *this bedroom has good energy*, or something. *If you would like to try it out*. What does it matter?" My husband backed away from her and politely suggested that our family might not need her services after all.

Or maybe they slept together in that ranch house. Maybe usually moral and righteous Victor couldn't resist such low-hanging fruit and let this forward, frothy agent suck him off in the slatted light of cheap blinds. Maybe they fucked in the bedroom closet, so hard they both left with rug burns. It's a little bit fun to feel the pain when I picture it.

But anyway, I have to retrieve Lucy from Danielle's. I brush the dirt off my jeans. I'm about to declare the binocular case a goner—we may or may not find it, but we definitely won't find it by despairing with shovels in our yard—when Marco comes through the back gate.

"We were just talking about you," Victor says, smiling his big, fake, flashy smile. Marco nods.

"I think I left my drill," he says.

"You didn't," Victor says. "There's no drill in there."

"I think I left it under the sink," Marco says. "I'm just going to go check."

"Did you fix the hole under there?" Victor asks. He stands, finally flicks the dirt off his face. I watch the fleck fly off and vanish before it ever hits the ground.

"Basically," says Marco.

Victor follows him up the stairs and into the house, legs a little stiff, head down like a domineering dog.

I put the tools back in the shed. Two crows scream above the walnut tree.

I'd be lying if I said I didn't, occasionally, follow Marco's fantasy to its logical conclusion. I descend the staircase in a negligée or whatever, leggings and a T-shirt. I walk close to him, and he reaches out and puts a warm, calloused palm on my lower back. Then his hands are everywhere at once, up my stomach and over my breasts—which are my old breasts, my pre-baby breasts that spring from my bony ribs. I watch his face as he looks at them, these breasts that could be in glossy magazines. And I tear his plaid shirt without worrying about how much it costs or how to sew the buttons back. His pecs look like rolling hills of sand dunes and the smell of him is not a smell so much as a cloud of sex. His finger slides into my underwear, where my vagina is still so very intact, not the scarred up and slightly intimidating place it became after Lucy's protracted entrance to the world.

"The hole under the sink must be redone," my husband says, "and the caulk's already come up. Why? What kind of caulk did you use?"

Marco looks studiously under the sink with a blankness as vast as the sea.

Danielle lives in the big lavender house at the end of the block, the kind of grand old house that used to stand alone overlooking farmland or some kind of estate, before all the smaller bungalows were built around it in the 1940s. Danielle is—and I'm not spinning yarns—a gasping expert. She used to do voice work in Hollywood until she became famous for expressing surprise. Now, apparently, she can freelance from Portland, flying out to Los Angeles to gasp every once in a while—an oral stunt man. Or it's something like that. Maybe I wasn't fully listening when she explained it to me. Though she's not yet thirty-four, she appears to be financially set, whether from the gasping or the divorce or an inheritance or a trust fund, I have no idea.

"Hi, Paige!" she says as she opens the door. She's wearing an oversized, mustard-colored sweater that looks like a thrift store find and probably cost three hundred dollars.

Her house, free of dust motes, cat hair, and the general detritus of modern life, always smells of lemons gently fading into some kind of sage or woodsmoke. Whenever we have Madeline over to our house, I become very aware of the rip in our secondhand tweed sofa and the vague smell of decaying food that emanates from our kitchen compost bin.

Lucy appears, a big brown splotch on her strawberry T-shirt. She's eating a piece of baguette.

"Brie," she says, opening the baguette and showing me a whitish lump. Then she briefly rests against my legs before darting off.

I follow Danielle into the kitchen. The girls have been playing with Madeline's all-wood, Waldorf-inspired dollhouse, complete with tiny, non-toxic beds and dressers. Lucy returns to it, kneeling in the corner of the living room where it sits upon a custom children's table with tiny elephants carved into the legs.

An indisputable fact: Lucy, my daughter, is so much prettier than Madeline. No matter our squat and dim house, our debris-strewn yard. Madeline has tight red curls and a soft, smeary nose with nostrils that you can see straight into. Probably, she looks like her father. Lucy, my brilliant, quick-witted child, has Victor's dark hair. The gloss in her nearly black eyes is like wet obsidian, deep and soulful and bright. And she moves with a gazelle's ease, this baby of mine, this sleek little girl. Sometimes I wish we had not been so old when we had her, but it had been an ordeal—two years of fertility doctors, a miscarriage, the whole nine yards. We were lucky, with my aging eggs and Victor's sleepy sperm, to have a child at all. Had I known the babies I was capable of producing, I might have started at twenty, had a whole army.

Danielle takes out a big wheel of brie, a bowl of cherries, and a plate of cured meats, half-eaten and covered in plastic wrap.

"Wow," I say. "You really know how to snack."

Danielle smiles with only half her mouth so that her dimple deepens into a black abyss.

Danielle is beautiful, too. People everywhere wave at her, smile, think they know her when, in fact, that's not why she caught their eye. Her huge forehead announces her thick, honey-colored hair that in some lights gives way to a strawberry blond. It's wavy, and she wears it in a nesty bun, with tendrils climbing down her neck as if she's a living, breathing sweet pea vine. She's not terribly thin—a refreshing trait in this city of bone-broth-sipping anorexics. Her curves just make her look sensual. She once told me she breastfed Madeline for thirty-one months. Men, babies, whole towns could probably live off that body for a while, so glossy with nutrients.

"So, how was the date?" I ask, glancing at the kitchen island, which does actually seem to be a little out of order, the basket of fruit moved near the toaster, a wadded towel by the knife block.

"The guy's great. So . . . attentive." She lowers her voice. "It's been a while. I thought I'd aged out of that kind of thing."

The girls come crashing into the kitchen with a bug net and a tiny doll that has gotten ensnared in the string. I take it and start to untangle her, but her tiny plastic fingers have something disgusting and sticky on them that's making the string come apart.

Danielle leans back slightly, hand on her lower back, as if to express that she's a little sore, what from all the contortions.

Danielle sees a feminist counselor via Skype, a woman who believes in Danielle's inborn human potential, her capacity to make a six-figure salary gasping, her inner magnetism that will attract a well-rounded and compassionate man. Six times a year, Danielle travels to a women's gathering in Ojai where they do things like talk to their ancestors in a hall of mirrors, thanking them and handing them unwanted baggage. They eat clean food and hike and sing and visualize themselves in fantastic futures. More than once, she's asked if I want to come with her. More than once, I have felt myself startle, as if she has offered to cover me in scalding glue. But Danielle *believes*—believes that you can manifest the good things in life through positive thinking, that her bad marriage resulted from her erroneous inner narrative. My mother, a botanist with a zest for life, a passion for Latin dance and freshwater pearls, died of a staph infection when I was ten. Enough said.

"Can I stay a little longer, Mom?" Lucy asks, holding the baguette. She hands me the brie. Danielle holds out her hand. She puts the white wad in the pristine compost container—handmade pottery—by her sink.

"I don't have that much going on," Danielle says. "She can stay. Madeline and I had planned to go the pool, but—"

"I want to go to the pool!" Madeline says.

"We have to find the binocular case, or your father may blow a gasket," I say to Lucy, because I can't think of another extraction technique.

"I know where that is," Madeline says.

"You do?" I say.

"Yeah," Madeline says. "We were playing with it the other day. We were making a mouse house."

"Oh yeah," says my daughter.

"Did you bury it?" I ask.

"No," says Madeline.

"Where is it?"

"Ummmm," Madeline says, making a cute face and tilting her head. "Um-mmmm," then she giggles.

"Would you be able to show me?" I ask.

"Ummmm," Madeline says again, trying to prompt me to smile at her as though she's the most astonishing delight. I give her the requisite smile. "I don't know," she says.

"We could walk over," Danielle says, "and you can see if you can remember. Then go to the pool after, okay Mads?"

"Is it in the backyard?" I ask as we near the house.

"Yeah," Madeline says. "I think so." I let the girls in through the back gate. Madeline rushes over to the birdbath in a corner of the yard covered in ivy. She starts rooting around. We already looked there.

Danielle keeps glancing toward the street, where Marco parked his gray truck, one wheel on the curb.

"Want a glass of water?" I ask. She follows me up the back stairs into the kitchen where Victor stands, holding a screwdriver. He gives me a look.

I met Victor one thousand years ago in San Francisco when we both worked at a bike co-op. He repaired bikes. I rang people up. Can that really be true? Did we used to sleep together on an old futon under a huge window overlooking Valencia Street, which was just butcher shops and thrift stores once upon a time? A friend recently sent me a picture of the old butcher shop, still a butcher shop, but now all wood and gleaming chrome with eleven-dollar-a-pound artisanal hot dogs.

I know the look, of course. It means, what a jackass; it means, I hate contractors; it means, I should kick this guy's ass. A small puddle of water has accumulated on our floor.

I've always loved my husband. Well, actually, at first I thought he was a tiresome pedant, inserting Marxist theory into every conversation. And then after a month or two of furtive make-out sessions in the repair room of the co-op, I loved him. He knew how to be still. He knew how to listen, even if he didn't always do it. Lying next to him after sex, I felt at ease, not filled with the sharp melancholy I'd previously known. And for a moment, watching him stand there with that screwdriver and that look, a tenderness fills me. It flares up whenever it wants, this alliance, this feisty monogamous urge.

And then the toilet flushes.

Marco rounds the bend to the kitchen, his face harboring shadows, deep in some argument with Victor. But then he notices Danielle, standing there like she's the rarest of buds, thrusting fresh and new out of that baggy outfit, holding the water glass in such a way that it reveals the loveliness of her wrists, and he halts, then does something surreptitious with his hands. He beams a smile at Danielle as he does it, but it doesn't distract me; he has removed his wedding band, slipped it into his pocket. Did Victor see it? Yes, absolutely.

"Oh!" Danielle says, and with this one utterance her breasts seem to enlarge, grow rounder, and she leans back on our counter, which is improperly grouted to the wall. Her neck, when she leans like this, exposes itself, so long and vulnerable and white.

"I didn't realize you were working over here at Paige and Victor's!" she says, and I scour my brain to remember what I've said about this terrible remodel. Surely I've bitched about it.

"Just finishing up the job," he says, which is interesting to hear.

I can see Victor putting it all together, even though I didn't tell him why Madeline spent the night. "You two know each other?" he asks.

Danielle pushes off the counter and yanks the clip out of her bun. Then she coils her hair again and fastens it tighter, no tendrils hanging down.

"We do," Danielle says.

Marco nods. "I was just finishing up here for the day," he says. "Want to walk me to my truck?"

Victor and I exchange a look that communicates pretty much everything that anyone would need to know about the current situation.

Danielle glances toward the back door. Outside, her daughter looks for the case with my daughter.

Danielle has told me a little bit about her ex, a Hollywood manager named Elijah, a charmer, a talker, though when at home alone with Danielle, he barely spoke. After she got pregnant, he wouldn't touch her.

Danielle told me this last summer. The girls played and we drank wine on her driveway, looking at the flowers she'd planted in the new garden boxes.

"That must have been terrible," I said, and she looked down the street and began openly weeping.

I didn't know what to do. How do you deal with people like this, so quick to feel their feelings, as if they curate and file them carefully so that whenever they think a thought, they can find the corresponding emotion? I can't even begin to imagine how exhausting that must be. I put my hand on her arm, though really, I wanted her to give me more details: a fecund and nubile Danielle, her round belly harboring kicking, squirming life, her whole body pounding with the need to fuck—on the ground, in the bed, doggy style, pretzeled up, her pregnancy hormones giving her clitoris a new and defiant will of its own, and this husband tensing up, curling his lip as if her vagina had an odor. Masturbating into rags that he let her find and toss into the hamper.

"God," Danielle said, gazing at her black-eyed Susans, her bluebells, and her daisies. I waited for her to continue, to tell me that it had hurt to be rejected but she'd learned to love herself, or learned that motherhood was worth it, or learned whatever it is—whatever made the whole thing feel epiphanic—but she never finished the thought. Instead, she excused herself, turned and started to walk inside the house, stepped in something, kicked off her sandal, sniffed and sighed and, with the stick of a child's pinwheel that had been spinning in the flowerbed, dislodged a piece of cat shit from the sole.

That night, I slid Victor's boxers down and imagined Danielle, pregnant and randy, tits heavy with the anticipation of milk, belly a vein-streaked orb, as Victor pressed himself into me. When I came, I imagined her coming, the way her face might look, sweaty and pink, that pretty hair stuck to her neck.

"I'd love to have another baby," she'd told me on another morning, as Madeline and Lucy put on their shoes in my hallway.

"Still plenty of time," I said to her, and she smiled and nodded, and that night I cut my hand chopping tomatoes, a deep gash that stained my white shorts and made me so angry I could barely bandage it up.

"I can walk you out, sure," Danielle says, a little too fast. She sets the glass on the counter. Marco nods at Victor.

"Hey," Victor says. He points at the water on the floor. "You can't leave a leaking pipe until tomorrow."

"Oh, I can't work tomorrow," says Marco. "I'll have to turn the water off at the source and come back Tuesday."

"It's the *kitchen sink*," says Victor. "You need to fix the pipe." Victor's face is starting to get red above his dark beard.

Marco shrugs.

"What kind of contractor leaves a puddle of water on the kitchen floor for days on end. In a house that is lived in? In a house with a child? I'm sick of this shit, Marco. You'll stay here until the sink works. And then you'll finish the rest of this work and clean the fucking yard."

I glance at Danielle, chin angled down now, her neck no longer the focal point. Will she gasp?

"Look, man," Marco says, "this kitchen is totally functional. And the demo was a lot more work than I thought. And you got a good price. If you want more done, we can renegotiate. But you can't be cheap. I need to eat, too."

"Functional? What does functional mean to you? Generally, to most of the world, it means that things function."

Once, when we were living in Hayes Valley, a meth-addled lunatic leapt out from behind a building and grabbed my breasts. Victor punched him in the face, just like that. The world turned a sparkling aquamarine when he did it. I felt so loved, which was not the reaction I meant to have.

"I did everything I was contracted to do. That light wasn't in the bid. And the sink would work except you have bad pipes, and that wasn't in the bid either. I'd need to add several hundred for parts and labor. Closer to a thousand, actually. And I can't do it right now, man."

"We hired you to remodel the kitchen. The lights and sink and counters were definitely in the bid. Don't get screwy with me, *man*. I'm just not in the mood."

Marco moves his shoulders back. All the little synapses in his brain flick and dance. But he can't think of what to say.

"I'm finished with this job," says Marco. "I quit."

"You *quit?*" says Victor. "You can't quit. You have a contract and our money. I'll alert the contractor's board. Go ahead and try to quit."

"I'm—" Danielle starts. She's doing something funny with the heels of her palms, pressing them together. "I'm . . . sure you can find a way to resolve this. What exactly is the problem?"

"We found the bird!" says Lucy, bursting through the back door. Then I see the dead bird in her hands.

"Oh, Jesus, Lucy!" I pull the cabinet open to pull out the trash bin and the hinge breaks.

"You couldn't even make this shit up," says Victor.

"Those were the hinges in the bid," says Marco, his lips so soft above that blond goatee he's nurturing, that little patch of fur he probably dragged into Danielle's private swamps last night, his chin as obdurate as any child's. "You could have chosen classier things," he says.

Victor puts the screwdriver down.

"You want to talk about classy?" says Victor. He stands too straight, a little too close to Marco, who also stands too straight. "Why don't you show your girlfriend here your wedding ring."

Marco's head angles back from his neck, his chin juts. And for a minute, the pair of them stand like that.

The night that Victor's half-brother came for dinner with the expensive wine, I made spaghetti and cleaned the house as Victor played airplane with

Lucy with a little too much gaiety. The spring night air flirted, the crocus buds in the yard poked their heads from glistening soil, a light rain hit the roof, and the brilliant green moss sang its color to the world.

I could see some similarities between Quinn and Victor, as we sat there in the flickering candlelight. Their hands, for example, had the same tulip-shaped fingernails and oddly angled thumbs. And there was a resemblance across the brow and in the curve of the nostrils. But Quinn was much smaller in stature, with reedy bones and sandy-colored hair. We all pretended that the dinner had no bizarre undertones as we discussed Quinn's law firm and Victor's job at the environmental nonprofit, the dire political landscape and the climate.

"You didn't miss much," Quinn finally said. Lucy had gone to bed. The wine glasses looked frosted with fingerprints, the dishes mostly cleared. "He was the worst—my mother got a little inheritance from her father's printing business after he died, and he convinced her to let him put it into his self-produced country album." He reached for his phone and showed Victor a photo of it, a man's bearded face garlanded by roses, the lighting soft, his name in hot pink gothic font at the bottom: EDDIE JOEL DUSSEL. "Of course it made no money, though he bankrupted us making, like, ninety-five thousand cassette copies and mailing them all over the world. One station played his song, "Roses and Poses" as a joke and he flew into a rage, breaking the door off our fridge. My mother had no spine—took him back, took him back. Finally, he ran off with some guitar student of his, barely eighteen. They had a daughter, Ocean Wave Dussel—she's twenty-two now. I tracked her down, too, in a prison in Indiana."

I'd never seen the look that came across Victor's face before, and I've never seen it since. It made me stand up and put my hands on his shoulders, then on his chest. He didn't reach for me.

"Sounds rough, Quinn," I said.

"Oh, you know," Quinn said. "You have to play with the hand you're dealt. I just wanted you to know. I just thought, probably, you wondered what you missed. I would have. And I'm here to tell you, it wasn't anything. Just a frustrated, damaged asshole with efficient sperm."

And then he gave Victor the binoculars and the book. For about a month, the binoculars lay in the corner of the dining room. Then one day, I noticed them in the bedroom. Then in the closet. Then we both noticed them in Lucy's room.

The men face each other and I'm tempted to laugh, to break the tension somehow. Marco's puffed himself up so he's almost as tall as Victor. His blond hair stands off his head. Did he really meet Danielle through mutual friends? The idea of Marco with friends amuses me. What does he do for fun? Play kickball? Race go-karts? I'd only ever imagined him skulking home to his wife, the caustic things the wife would say, the silence he'd use like a barricade. But surely he owns other outfits, not just Carhartts.

Marco takes a step back and punches Victor in the face.

I don't know who gasps with more authority, me or Danielle. But Lucy yelps and covers her face with her hands and Madeline, strangely, claps her hands, just once, but loudly.

I jump toward Victor, but he's calmly taking out his cell phone. So I go to Lucy and pick her up. She presses her face into my neck, but quickly pulls back to stare at the men.

"I'm sorry, man, I'm sorry," says Marco. He's red and his hands are shaking. "I lost my temper, man."

While Marco watches, Victor narrates the situation to the police. Assault, he calmly says. Punched by the contractor, Marco Schumaker. He gives our home address.

Danielle holds Madeline close, her beautiful mouth twisting downward, seeing that she will, again, go to sleep on her fancy sheets alone. Marco pleads with Victor not to talk to the cops. He promises to finish the sink, to upgrade the hinges. Says something about a kickback and fifteen percent. The dead bird rests on top of an egg carton and some plastic wrap. I wonder, for the first time, if the binoculars even had a case. Now that I think about it, I can see Quinn handing them to Victor with nothing around them.

Lucy continues to watch her father. Her stoic daddy with the same eyes as she has looks as tall as Paul Bunyan, his back straight and long. As he stands there, not talking, Marco yammers. Soon, in the cartoon of Lucy's retelling, Marco will be the size of a doll, then the size of a mouse, then he will not be there at all.

When Lucy was small, Victor spent every morning with her, reading to her, singing to her, dancing to the Cure or Prince. He never traveled. He never missed a morning. He still looks her straight in the eyes when he talks to her. *Dada* was her first word. Even though it annoyed me, I could understand the depth of his pride.

Tonight, Victor will explain to her that some people are assholes. He will make her white teddy bear do the cha-cha. And then he will eventually come to bed, and we'll go over this day, and I'll talk him out of pressing charges.

I look at the bird. It's pretty, with its grayish tufts and its tiny yellow beak. I have no idea what kind of bird it is. Some backyard dweller, ubiquitous, food for the hawks and cats. So close at hand, you wouldn't need binoculars to find it.

DO
THE DEAD
GRIEVE

At seventy-four, my father bought an expensive carbon bicycle in order to keep up with his spin instructor girlfriend. Belinda biked many miles a day for fun, in addition to the miles she racked up teaching, trying to outrun the calories that threatened to stick to her sculpted little body. She biked up hills and down them, across cities, along the wide rivers that run through our state. And my father, on one of these trips with her, going down a very large hill, possibly a small mountain, lost control of the bicycle. He probably didn't know not to squeeze the front brakes of such a light bike while careening downhill, and he sailed up and over it, like an aerial gymnast. He landed on his side and because Belinda was way ahead of him, miles ahead, burning off the half a muffin she'd eaten, she had no idea that he'd cracked half the ribs in his chest.

A passerby stopped, called an ambulance, and my father spent a month in the ICU on paralytics and a ventilator, his fingers losing their tenuous grip on the cliff that was his life.

I'd lost my mother fifteen years before to cancer. And I had no other living family. Plus, I was seven months pregnant. I spent those ICU months in a state of extreme anxiety and tension, studying the research of flail chests and sudden acute respiratory syndrome, while trying to sleep and eat for the sake of my unborn daughter. And one night, shortly after the accident when his prognosis had worsened from an eighty percent chance of dying to nearly a hundred, I went to my father's house to get something—papers? A cord? And I found myself so fatigued, I could do nothing but sink to the bed.

It was the same bed, the same mattress, the very spot where my mother died, where her spirit or soul or whatever animated her in life suddenly departed and left only a waxen, silent replica.

I lay in bed and felt the baby moving, using her little heels to dig into the edge of my ribcage and propel herself toward my pelvic area, where she'd bonk her head and start over. She liked to do this, and I liked to feel it. It felt like our own private language. In that state of exhaustion, with my baby working out her thighs and my father hovering between life and death, I drifted into a state near sleep, an open and receptive state. And my mother came into the room.

I'd seen her in this way before, but not for over a decade, and only in Berkeley, where I lived in the years following her death. She'd sometimes come and sit with me on my bed in the morning, just before I truly woke. But eventually I moved north and she stopped visiting. I imagine it got too difficult to come to me, and her afterlife, whatever it was, absorbed her. I imagined the spirit world bustling with activity, offering new dramas and distractions. Or maybe it was something else entirely, something I couldn't imagine, that took her away. Strong winds beyond the Bardo. Or a visitation punch card.

Feeling her there, a frost I hadn't realized encased me began to melt. And as it melted, all of this . . . energy . . . or hurt or want or something vital came off me like vapor.

I felt rudderless without a mother as I positioned myself to cross that threshold into motherhood myself and she must have sensed this.

Mom, I said to her. The blunt and sudden sound of my voice seeming to bounce against that angled ceiling.

I expected the connection, the warmth of her brown eyes meeting mine, the feeling of being entirely known. Though not a perfect mother, she'd been a real mother, a flawed and judgmental person who loved me forcefully and truly.

But she didn't come to me. She glanced at me from the ceiling where she hovered. I couldn't see her. Or, I did see her, but without my eyes. It's hard to explain. I could tell she meant business. "Oh," she said. "I was looking for

DO THE DEAD GRIEVE

your father." My hands did not move from their perch on my daughter. "I've come to get him."

Everything stopped—the heat, the warmth, even the exhaustion. My adrenaline coursed. I sat up. My baby stopped kicking. The world around me went hazy and yet my thoughts felt so very sharp. I knew what she meant. I could feel what trailed behind her: a death-fog.

"No," I said, sitting up in the bed. "I'm pregnant. I'm about to have a baby. You can't take him right now. Please don't take him. It's terrible timing."

The little green light from my father's ancient tape player alarm clock glowed, the numbers changing. Only six o'clock at night, but the room was dark and closed and spinning, sort of, though not spinning exactly. Still, it didn't feel like a normal room in a normal house, not at that moment. A charge shot through the air. And my mother stopped, her attention now on me. But it wasn't the attention I craved, the maternal depth of love, the scooping up and holding close, the whispering of encouragement I fantasized about. Instead, she assessed the situation, seemed to ask herself in a lawyerly way, whether she could live (live?) with herself if she took my father now. I could hear her give a gruff sigh, and then she disappeared. The room went plain again. The heat rumbled on—the first cold day of fall, and the small cord on the blinds shuddered with the blowing air.

The next day, my father made a miraculous turnaround. The fluid in his lungs began to clear. The doctors seemed close to ecstatic. What had happened? It must have been the steroids. About two weeks later, the doctors released him to a rehab center. A miracle. Everyone said as much. The world had given us a gift, or at least taken away a tragedy. Three weeks after that, I gave birth to Janie.

It was such a crazy time. Everything ended up falling into a soupy moat—my father's accident, Belinda's cavalry of dysfunction (we now no longer spoke), even my former life. The days turned into ninety-minute segments of pumping, nursing, and trying to rest as this new life squirmed and screamed, and I attempted to keep up with my emotions, which vacillated between a vacancy and delirious affection, dipping every so often into irrational exhausted fury, but even this had nowhere to land, as I wasn't sleeping, and in that state, nothing whatsoever lands. And eventually, Janie became a baby, not so much a newborn, and I slept a few hours, and understood day and night, and answered some emails, and my father came to visit, driving the two hours north alone, limping into the house exhausted and so much older than he had been, but sometimes filled with earnestness I hadn't seen in him before. "I was basically dead and I didn't die," he said. "And now I have to try to live as though I were given a second chance."

He painted his house. He redid his deck. He trained his dog. He donated money to various causes. He held Janie as though she had fallen from the sky and might break.

The day of the accident, I'd raced to the hospital. The doctors met me in the waiting area with a series of release forms. But Belinda wouldn't allow the doctors to talk. "This can't be happening to me," she kept saying. "It's not my fault. He probably had a brain aneurism." Finally, the doctors grew irritated and asked her if she could please step aside and let them talk to the family.

"I am family," she said. "I am basically the wife!"

This hadn't been my understanding of their situation.

I did my best to ignore her in the days that followed, as she inserted herself into every scenario, though the sight of Belinda, sitting like an injured queen on the upholstered bench in the hospital room made my fists ball. Every day, she erased my name and phone number from the family contact list near the hospital bed and wrote her own. When I arrived, I erased her name. And on and on. Eventually, we ceased talking. She lurked in the hospital halls, waiting for me to leave so that she could resume her widow's perch on the bench.

When he finally felt better, or at least well enough to talk and walk with a walker, he claimed he no longer wished to traffic in such dysfunction. He understood Belinda to be deeply selfishness (she relished the attention she received while he lay dying, but when they discharged him and he truly needed help, she disappeared to have elective surgery). But, he couldn't seem to shake her. He'd tell her he felt differently now and she'd cry and threaten him. She promised change. She hung on. And when he relented, a honeymoon phase would follow during which she'd pour little poisons in his ear about me. Occasionally my father told me these things—that she claimed I lied about her behavior in the hospital, that she might have the stronger mind for power of attorney over him, and I'd hate her a little bit more. But I couldn't focus on this bag of bones on her fancy bicycle. I had a new baby, a husband with a taxing job, a miracle father I nearly lost, and four hours of sleep a night. Besides, I was my father's only daughter, and Janie his only granddaughter. Belinda could bike to Alaska and back, contort herself sexually in little outfits that suggested she'd retained the curves of her sex, but she'd never produce more actual family. I held the ultimate trump card in my arms every day, nearly every hour of every day, this wiggling, energetic, buzzy little dark-haired baby whose future spread out before her, I hoped, like a dazzling array of gems.

This kind of love felt so exotic, so singular. I'd birthed the perfect human being, unblemished and bright and silly, velveteen and glossy with human newness. I'd brought her forth, and the strangeness of that, and the depth of my feelings, belonged only to us.

Winter arrived, and that year it snowed and snowed, a rare occurrence in our city, and Janie got a very bad cold. I stayed up, tending to her, and in the middle of one of these long, difficult nights, I opened her tiny closet and experienced it again, the presence of my mother.

Overjoyed to see her, I felt a leaping, a heat.

"Rebecca," she said. I waited for it like a starving person waiting for bread—her warm and focused love. The extension of this love to Janie. I couldn't breathe or speak.

"I can't wait anymore," she said. "It's too hard."

Invisible vectors pinned me in place.

"Please tell your father that I'm sorry."

"What do you mean?" I whispered. And Janie stopped fussing as if to listen.

"Mom?"

I'd put an old photograph of her in Janie's room, my mother as a chubby toddler, peering over the cowlicked head of her baby brother. Now, she hovered right next to it. She'd once been a child, a baby like Janie, and now she was a ghost. Pieces of her life littered this bedroom in Portland. She leapt to life in me every time I read Janie one of the picture books she'd carefully saved from my childhood or petted Janie's head, the way she used to pet mine. And when she looked at us, she probably saw pieces of her mother, too, and on and on and on.

"I can't really explain it all," she said. "I can't stay that long. And I probably couldn't explain even if I wanted to. But he'll know when he gets here. I'm not coming to get him. But I also won't wait."

I reached into the closet for the burp cloths I'd opened it to find. Did I think I could grab her? I didn't grab her.

"I've been trying to get to him, but I can't. He doesn't see me because he's so caught up in his own drama with that ridiculous girlfriend of his. It would be different if he were happy. This would be easier to do. He'd maybe have somewhere else to go." I felt her attention drift, almost like she had a phone. But then, "He's not young by any stretch of the imagination, you know. And he's going to waste the rest of his time muddled up in that ambivalence. What I would have done with another decade! But, it's his to spend. And I can't cut through it. It's exhausting to try."

The line had a weird echo in my mind. And it distracted me just enough that I lost her. Janie started up again, shrieking this time, and rubbing her back didn't cut it, so I held her and rocked her and shushed her and sang those songs my mother sang to me, those words her mother probably sang to her, old show tunes and lullabies, and I didn't have time to consider what she'd said, or why there'd been an echo, until later when a babysitter came so that I could sleep and I crawled into bed and remembered that my father had said this very same thing to me, shortly after his release from the hospital. "I want to end things with Belinda, but it's just too exhausting to try." And maybe there was a weird windiness in his kitchen at that moment, like someone else was listening, but I chalked it up to the out of body experience

I had whenever my father expressed even halfhearted loyalty to a woman who wished, with such singlemindedness, that I did not exist.

How exactly was I supposed to relay this message to my father? And what exactly was the message? What did it mean? And so, I did nothing, because I had no idea how to play this card, whatever it was. It seemed unfair to give me the card in the first place.

And then one night I woke up with a high-pitched feeling. I'd had a dream about her, a nightmare I hadn't had for years, that she wasn't actually dead, that she'd simply moved to Florida to be with another man. I ran into her in the airport and she acknowledged and dismissed me in one quick glance. And in the shaky space after the dream, I remembered the email.

I got up, left my husband snoring quietly beside me, trying not to creak our ancient floors as I made my way past Janie's nursery to my laptop.

Many months prior, during the bicycle crisis, I'd received an email, out of the blue, from a man named Harold Levin. He told me he'd known my mother long ago, when they were both in college and one day he thought to look her up and found her obituary. It made him extremely sad to learn that her life had been cut short, he wrote. And he wanted to reach out to tell me what a remarkable and brilliant young woman my mother had been. "She was also beautiful, strikingly so," he wrote. "And probably the smartest woman I have ever met." I'd replied with a polite "thank you for writing," which inspired him to compose a much longer, more florid note to me. "I was wildly in love with your stunning mother," he wrote. "We had a brief love affair. She could sing like an angel. She starred in every play, wrote songs for the sorority. What a mind! What a spirit! I wanted to marry her, but she only had eyes for the older boys. She was so mature, and I was just a little doofus at the time. Still, I have never stopped thinking about what our lives could have been. If only."

I hadn't written back to him. But I remembered my mother mentioning something about a man from when she was younger—what had she said? Her coyness annoyed me at the time. I didn't want to think about my mother involved in some carnal fling back when she lived in an apartment in Manhattan a thousand years before I existed. And it seemed like she wanted me to ask questions so that she could make a smug little face, and I hadn't wanted to see it.

I'd Googled the guy when I got this second email. He had gray hair and a beard and worked in medical marketing.

I found his Facebook profile again and stared. A stream of recent condolence notes littered the page. Apparently, he'd just died. Pancreatic cancer, swift and surprising. I followed a link and learned he'd long been divorced, and left behind one child, a son, Uri Allen Levin. I shut my laptop.

So, there it was. Or was it? Had my mother come to tell me that she'd decided to run off into the afterlife with Harold Levin?

After my mother's death, I wondered for hours on end what had become of her. I imagined her caught between worlds in a static-filled, windy intermediate zone, trying to stay my mother as forces pulled her from me. I decorated this in my mind, tried in vain to see it, this sightless world of the dead. I imagined my grandfather and grandmother there with her. But that never felt quite right. I pictured her alone, fighting some kind of battle in an in-between place.

I tried to channel her, to wish her next to me, but I never succeeded. If she came, she came; it had nothing to do with my wishing. The living, it seemed, had no power in this regard, but she still maintained a kind of hold over me. I still pined for her, made decisions hoping she'd know.

But the longer she stayed dead, the more loyalties rearranged themselves. Now, I had Janie. I had Noah, my husband. I no longer had time to imagine her whereabouts.

And for the first time, I wondered if she noticed that. And if the dead, as they recede from the minds of the living, grieve, too.

"Please tell him I'm sorry," my mother had said. She couldn't wait. I'd been born early. I couldn't wait. Janie, now six months old, already assumed a crawl position, her brow serious, her determination palpable. The women in my family were all born impatient. Little fires in their bellies blown about by their own hot breath.

My father, on the other hand, I'm not sure I would call him patient so much as stoic. He didn't have a fire in his belly. I imagined it more like a factory in there, churning and efficient. When my mother died, he didn't cry. He hung his head and shook his head and held his head, as if his head itself were the key to surviving. And then he put one foot in front of the other and bedded several much younger women, all of them ambivalent, all of them fascinating to him until they left him for younger men. And then he found Belinda, and now here we all were.

Uri Levin, Harold Levin's son, kept a blog. A little younger than me, and an aspiring naturalist, he had some sort of day job I couldn't figure out. He lived outside of Joshua Tree, in the Palm Desert. He featured many photos of his wife, Alyssa, and mentioned that they had been unable to have a child of their own, despite intervention. They'd decided not to go broke trying for a baby. Instead, they had three dogs, all of them rescues. Most of the blog would have bored even the most stalwart reader of nature writing—tangled descriptions of the pine trees that went on for paragraphs, summaries of environmental news, maudlin musings about climate change, gratitude that he had no human offspring to subject to such a future. But I gravitated to the parts about his father.

His father called him one morning complaining of pain in his stomach, and when he finally went to get it checked out, he learned that he had advanced metastatic cancer and less than three months to live.

"My dad in his happy place," Uri wrote under a photo of Harold Levin in a lush garden. Harold had loved his son with the same effusive manner he displayed in his emails. He'd called Uri every few days for his whole adult life. I scoured the blog looking for a sign I felt certain would come.

But, nothing. Just the dogs and desert, occasionally Alyssa with her colorful scarf and bowls of soup, her fresh baked bread, blah blah blah. These were not the things I was after.

"This is kind of awkward," said Noah one night, he with his iPad and I with my *New Yorker*. "But who's Uri Levin?"

"What?" I asked.

"You loaned me your laptop and I was trying to find an article in the browsing history, and I noticed that you've been on Uri Levin's blog every single day." Raised well by confident parents, Noah rarely got jealous or suspicious. He believed in his own goodness, and as an extension, believed in mine. I could feel this in his presence, a gentleness that every so often annoyed me. I tried to explain it. Noah listened in the dim light in his worn T-shirt, his stubble flecked with gray. I'd told him about the visitation in my father's house, to which he'd ascribed to lack of rest, fear, grief, and hormones, and now I told him about the second visitation and the email from Harold Levin that I hadn't thought to mention during my dad's hospitalization. I told him about how I'd recently discovered that Harold Levin had died around the same time that my mother had come to me to tell me she wouldn't wait for my father, and that I felt certain that that was what she'd been trying to explain, and that when my father finally died, he wouldn't be able to simply go to my mother, because she had changed teams. My father would have to float around the afterlife, a lonely, forlorn ghost.

I grew animated trying to explain it, lost in the details of each scene, and when I finally finished, Noah looked at me with such gravity.

"I don't think you are getting enough sleep," he said.

"I think I need to tell my dad, though," I said.

"Yeah," said Noah, touching his stubble. "But wait, why are you obsessing about Uri Levin?"

"He seems like a key," I said.

"A key."

"Well, I don't know. I wondered if maybe he'd heard from his dad. And maybe his dad mentioned my mom."

Noah looked down at his lap, at the dark iPad sitting on it. He pressed the little button to light up the screen, but he didn't read the article. He looked at me.

"Are you saying that you're waiting for corroborating evidence before you tell your dad that your mom came to kill him but decided against it and now isn't going to wait for him in the afterlife because she's shacked up with an old boyfriend, and so his choice is . . . to drop dead and duke it out or be alone for eternity?"

"No," I said. I worried the edge of my magazine. "Well, I don't know. He might have other options."

"Do you think your dad should have died, too? Do you want him to be dead with your mom instead of alive with Belinda?"

"No," I said. "I don't want him to be dead."

"I'm not sure I understand where you're going with any of this," Noah said. "I think you should get some rest. If Janie wakes, I'll deal with it. Put in ear-plugs."

Of course I was tired. I had a six-month-old who still woke at night, who wanted action and songs and outside time and to move and dance and move some more. This baby hungered for life, sucked it down like Jello shots, lit up when things got wild—a band played, a bunch of birds fluttered. This baby was drunk with living.

And she made me drunk with living, too, even if I felt a fuzz in my cerebral cortex, like cotton had spread around in there. I breathed her in. I sucked her down into my lungs and something expanded even as the world contracted. Mothers understood this, probably, this contracting of the self, of the mind, and expansion of something we have no words for. I couldn't explain this to Noah either. But I didn't feel crazy or deluded or that kind of tired. I felt like a mother who had once had a mother and now did not.

Dear Uri,
You probably will think this is weird, but your father contacted me a while back, out of the blue, to reminisce about his relationship with

my mother when they were young. I started thinking about the email recently, and noticed he'd since passed away. I wanted to extend my condolences to you, just as your father extended his condolences to me. And to see if you ever wanted to talk about your father and my mother.

Sincerely,

Rebecca Rosenthal

The email whooshed and disappeared.

"It would be nice if Belinda could meet Janie," my father said. We were in my dining room. Noah had taken the opportunity to go for a run, so it was only me and my father and Janie, who looked stuck in crawl position on her foam tiles, staring at some photos I'd taped to the floor for her.

"Does Belinda want to meet Janie?" I asked.

"Who wouldn't want to meet Janie?" he said.

"Is she going to apologize to me?"

"She doesn't think she owes you an apology."

"Of course she doesn't."

"We could just let bygones be bygones."

"We could," I said. "But really, we won't."

My father pressed his lips together but didn't move. "Well," he said, "you could just let me take the baby to Belinda if you don't want to see her."

I sat dumbly on my chair for a moment. Was he serious? What did he imagine? That he'd borrow Janie, cart her off to Belinda's lace-infused split-level, the two of them doting on her, laughing with their heads tossed back in a fantasy of youthful parenthood? And to think he wanted to take my baby, my Janie, my drunk-with-living new glossy girl, to a woman that seemed to court death with every move she made. My hands clutched at each other. My baby put her hand in her mouth and chewed on it.

"Are you serious? Tell me you're not serious. You don't even have a car seat." Which wasn't what I wanted to say. And saying things I didn't even want to say made me even more tense. "Janie is mine. I made her. I carried her. I birthed her. My baby. She comes with me. And if Belinda doesn't like that, and doesn't want to apologize, then Belinda will just have to be content dividing her grapes in half or whatever she does with her time."

My father's eyes bulged a little. Mine probably did, too.

"Also, how serious are you and Belinda, anyway? I thought you wanted to break up with her."

"I do want to break up with her," my father said.

"Then why don't you?"

My father sat there, his face grayer than it had been moments before.

It felt wrong to see his vulnerable side, his fear of being alone. Outside the window, a neighbor's car wouldn't start.

"Do you ever think about Mom?" I finally asked.

"Of course," he said.

"Do you ever feel like you can still talk to her?"

"Talk to her?"

"Yeah. Like, do you ever feel her presence?"

He made the face he made when someone revealed intellectual frailty, a remote sadness about the feebleness of man.

"I sometimes feel her presence," I said.

"Yeah, well," he said. "If your mother ever did come back from the dead, she'd come straight to you."

"Why wouldn't she go straight to you?" I asked.

"I need to use the restroom," my father said, and he stood up. As soon as he rounded the corner, Janie put one hand out, then followed it with her knee, then the other hand and the other knee, and I yelled for my father to come see. She made her way to the cat's water bowl and plunged her hands into it, delightedly, so delightedly. Oh, my daughter and her endless delight.

My father didn't push the Belinda thing. More months passed. Janie grew out of her clothes and I bought her new clothes and she grew out of those. She began to eat foods—soups and stews and fruit and eggs, gobbling it all like she gobbled everything, and then one morning I found myself throwing up into the bushes on a walk with Janie.

That night, in the bathroom, staring first at the test strip and then at the heating vent, I tried to channel her. *I'm having another baby!* I told her.

The heating vent said nothing to me. Mildew crept darkly up the shower curtain.

How wild that life animated you, then passed through you this way. It poured this bounty over you but gave you no real understanding of any of it, just the thing itself.

I imagined my mother in the afterlife, in a celestial elevator with Belinda. My mother faced her, eyes penetrating, short hair blown about by the winds that always raged there. "She's my baby," my mother said to Belinda. "That daughter of his. My baby."

"Mom," I said to the bathroom.

"I never had a dad," Belinda said to my mom. "She can't have everything, all the time."

And there, in front of my mother, she devolved into a young woman with anxious dark eyes, then a teenager with running shorts, then a slightly fat girl in a pink dress, then a child with the sorrowful look of too much time alone. Then a baby in a baby chair, wailing and reaching for someone and my mother simply stood there, observing.

"You are not the child here," my mother said to her. But Belinda did not change back. Then Janie started crying down the hall.

Noah traveled again for his job. He went to Pakistan, then India, then Myanmar. He saw beautiful and horrible things, some of which he told me about. Janie pulled herself to standing. The new baby's heart began to beat. The new baby sprouted tiny arms and legs.

I did eventually receive a reply from Uri Levin.

Greetings, Rebecca,

Thank you for your note of condolence. This definitely has been a terrible time for us, and I miss my father every day.

I think I do remember my dad saying something about your mom.

But I'm afraid I don't remember much about it, just that he'd had some kind of crush on a girl back in Brooklyn. I suppose these things get lost in the extensive vaults of history. I am sorry, by the way, to hear of your mother's passing. May her memory be a blessing.

Sincerely,

Uri

I stared at the email. I attempted to draft a response. Dear Uri, Have you been in touch with your dead father? But everything I tried made me seem crazy, and maybe he didn't hold the key to anything, not even to his father's extensive vaults. Content to listen to the birds, feel the breeze on his skin, have no children. Content to type his homage to the earth as his life ticked steadily by.

Then one day, my father came again for dinner. He brought a casserole, but forgot it in the car. I watched him from my sofa spot as he slowly made his way down the steps. He opened his hatchback. He reached inside of it. He pulled out the pan and he shut the door and he started up the sidewalk again, so much older, so much stiffer than I would have pictured him.

Not yet part of the world, the baby in me had a future that my father no longer had. He'd take a first breath and a first step, lose a friend, fall in love. The world would belong to him, all of it novel and absorbing. And what if my father, whose firsts were mostly behind him, could just keep walking, could walk right through the line that separated us, the living from the dead. What if he carried that casserole straight through. If he crossed over tonight, would my mother still be waiting for him, holding out just a little bit longer? Would they eat grilled salmon, sip wine while my mother explained that he'd nearly missed the boat? Would he silently sit there, waiting for her soliloquy to end?

Oh, Mom. I wished that I could feel her. I wanted her hand on my head. Such a long time since I'd been her child.

My father stopped his glacial trek back to the door and took his cell phone out of his pocket, looking at it like it might spit out money. He answered a call. Undoubtedly Belinda. Noah plodded down the stairs toward me, holding Janie, just up from a nap. "Mama!" she squealed, reaching toward me.

"Baby," I said to her, receiving her stout little body in my arms, her strong limbs, always ready to reach, to pull, to push. I felt her hot breath, her sharp little nails against my cheek. "Baby Jane," I said to her, tickling her tummy. She arched back, screaming and giggling.

Maybe it had been too painful for my mother to keep coming to see me after she died. I don't know why that hadn't occurred to me before. She hadn't wanted to die. She repeated this so often, weeping into Kleenex as I sat there, young and scared and unable to respond.

She knew she had to leave a child on the earth, that she couldn't stay to protect, shield, or even comfort. Janie's soft lashes fringed large eyes, clearer and cleaner than glass, than a scalded needle, animated by the wonder of sight. Her baby skin, thin as parchment, revealed the veins and flush beneath. I smiled at her. She wrinkled her nose, showed her shiny gums and threw back her head, then brought it up and pressed her nose into mine.

To have to leave your child behind—even the thought of it—

I gathered Janie to me until she wriggled, trying to get free, intent on wreaking havoc on the bookcase, the toy basket, the bowl of Cheerios, the remote controls. Life! she said with her fat little hands. Life!

She tossed the first books to the rug, watched them land. And death disappeared backstage again, where I willed it to stay. Where it would stay, I suppose, until it didn't.

RADICAL
EMPATHY

The limo driver who picked Elisa up from the airport had a shaved head and a tattoo of Scrabble tiles across his neck, spelling MOTHER, as if the world were playing a joke. He checked her out before she crawled into the back, but he didn't say a word to her as they made their way across the freeways to their ultimate destination, a film studio in Beverly Hills.

At the security booth, Elisa got out of the limo, per the instructions in the egg broker's email. Then, another young man in a white linen button-down ushered her over to a golf cart. She took in what she could on their way to the trailer. Coffee carts and food carts and office buildings. An entire little town within gates, baking in a joyous bouncing sun.

Though the broker wouldn't tell her the name of the actress, a sign hung from the trailer door. Elisa felt a quick movement at the base of her throat, like the flicking open of a folding fan. The designer dress she'd borrowed from her roommate, Lena, strained a little around her ribs.

Marla Myles.

Elisa had allowed herself to imagine who the actress might be. A couple of weeks ago, the clinic called her to tell her that her profile had been select-ed. And not just by a wonderful family, by a notable family, a famous family. But before they could proceed, the actress wanted to actually meet her. An unusual request, but not out of the question when dealing with high profile clients, so long as they filled out the proper forms. Would she be amenable to such a meeting?

"You have to go," her friend Kia said, her laptop set over her legs like a tent. "Even if she decides not to pick you, you'd have the story for the rest of your life."

They sent her the forms, which included a nondisclosure agreement. She clicked through them, initialing the boxes, futzing with the signature box. Who would it be, this famous actress? A-list? B-list? Reality show nightmare? They wouldn't tell her in advance. The actress, apparently, wanted to be able to change her mind.

But Marla Myles, the regal, outspoken political activist and actress, star of serious dramas and indie films! Elisa couldn't believe it. This was a person who legitimately inspired admiration. An artist. A thinker. A person with whom she probably had actual things in common. Marla read. She did interviews in which she quoted Toni Morrison and Twyla Tharp.

A PA, a young man with a shiny mustache and white glasses, got her settled in the trailer. She sat on the leather loveseat, smoothed the red fabric of Lena's dress over her thighs.

The PA offered her a boxed sandwich which she declined. She gazed around. A pile of clothes on a dresser with piles of papers that were probably scripts. Mirrors propped against a wall.

"You must be Elisa!" Marla said, coming through the door in denim overalls, cuffs tucked into fancy cowboy boots with cutouts of moons and stars. She looked like she'd just rolled in, face free of make-up, hair frizzed.

Marla sat next to her on the sofa, smelling plain and clean. "I'm happy that you came all this way, and grateful," Marla said.

"Oh, I mean. Of course," said Elisa. Marla stared right into her eyes. Elisa made herself hold the gaze. As a woman navigating situations such as these, you were supposed to own your space. You were supposed to move less, uncross your arms.

Marla's eyes were blue, the same color as Elisa's, with a nearly identical pattern of brown islands. But they sat differently in her face, wider apart, with a high shine that seemed almost medicated. Her skin, too, didn't look real. Like a child's skin, it was uniform in color save for the slight blush of her cheeks, and as pure as the inside of a shell. Elisa's heart, god. It thudded around like a scared horse.

"I just want to thank you for coming all the way from Providence and during the semester. Brown! Such a good school. Do you love it?" Elisa smiled, nodded, but Marla kept talking. "It felt important for me to meet you—I hope you understand. It's a pretty big decision and I've been back and forth for, well, for a long time. I had this idea that we could spend the whole day together and I could really get to know you—what makes you tick, just all the stuff you can't really learn from the file. And maybe that would give me the courage. But, before we start I have to tell you, my day got sort of crazy. I have forty minutes before I have to go back to the set for this unexpected reshoot."

"Oh, okay. CliffsNotes version, then!" Elisa's voice was too high and perky. She felt stupid immediately, and crossed her arms, averted her eyes. But then, willing herself to rise to the occasion, said, "I can't believe *you're* the actress. I barely watch movies but I think I've seen most of yours."

Marla smiled a little more vividly.

"I loved *The Windy Creek Files*," Elisa said, remembering the bespectacled professor who assisted on cold cases. "And that indie film you did— what was it called? The one on the farm?"

"*Dreams of Horses*," Marla said, like she was answering a question at the DMV. Elisa's earlobes tingled. *Please don't let me be sick.*

"Tell me about your flight," said Marla. "Let's start there."

So, Elisa told her about getting a ride to the airport from Lena, her best friend, her roommate. Lena who was going to be a plastic surgeon because of her sister's cleft palate, because bringing someone normal function and beauty brought them possibility, too. She told her about the guy who drove her to the lot and his MOTHER tattoo. "Huh," Marla said, raising her perfect eyebrows.

What classes was she taking at Brown? Who did she love to read? What subjects felt most difficult? Would she describe herself as more logical or more imaginative? Did she finish the things she started? As Elisa answered the questions, she felt her nervousness subside. A regal stillness emanated from Marla. She leaned in to listen, laughed at jokes. She wanted to hear about the riding lessons Elisa took all through her childhood, dressage and then hunter jumping. In order to afford these lessons, Elisa's mother almost never bought anything for herself, wore the same winter coat as long as she could remember. Looking back, she could see the sacrifice, though at the time she'd just wanted a horse of her own and felt cheated that she'd never have one. She used to read the horse classifieds aloud as her mother made dinner. She talked about horses for too long. She saw Marla covertly glance at the clock.

Marla pulled a small bag of almonds from her purse and handed Elisa a couple.

"What made you offer your eggs?" she asked. "I mean, I know you answered that in your beautiful essay, but I feel like I'd rather hear it from you. It's a big deal—a lot of medication, shots, surgery. What prompted you to be so generous?"

Elisa had had to answer this question a number of times—in the interview with the broker, in the conversation with the counselor that screened her. In her donor info essay, she'd written about her aunt, Serena, who couldn't have kids.

What she hadn't said was that eggs from a girl like her went for a lot. With the fifty thousand dollars they promised her, she could take an internship upon graduation next year without worrying about accruing even more debt. She didn't want to be a doctor, a corporate lawyer, a software developer. She wanted to be a book editor. Her student loans, she worried, would dog her to her grave. But with a little lubricating cash, she could at least afford to worry less.

She read the ad in the *Brown Daily Herald* aloud to Lena. *ISO Ivy League Eggs*. So absurd! Ivy League eggs! People were so stupid with their misplaced ambitions and class-steeped narcissism. The eggs didn't have tiny little CVs. The eggs didn't row crew, didn't project natural charisma. Lena's brother, Paulson, worked at a bar in Northampton and showed no signs of being the least bit curious or ambitious. He barely got through high school. And he had the same genes as magna cum laude Lena. To pay double for such an egg! But Lena didn't smile.

The world would continue to be all fucked up, Lena believed, until each person stripped themselves of ego, of preconception, and began to mother one another, offering the kind of unconditional love so many had never received. She talked about this frequently, boldly, never worrying about how she appeared. And somehow she never appeared sanctimonious or overly earnest.

Lena with her disorderly long blond curls, her intense dark eyes, her square shoulders and precise enunciation. She wore jeans made out of thick denim that never sagged, perfectly faded military style coats. She came from the Upper West Side, her mother the granddaughter of a shipping magnate, her father some kind of financier. Lena didn't try to hide this, but she had a different way about her than most of the prep school kids who spent their time partying and networking and vacationing on Martha's Vineyard. So smart, she could slice through any idea, even the most stubbornly academic, to reveal its urgency and heart. She disdained the easy irony so many of their classmates relied upon. Just a way to shield the heart. Her boyfriend, Raj Singh, visited every weekend from Yale. He dreamed of bringing portable medical devices to war-ravaged countries.

The two of them, Lena and Raj, would open their hearts and never turn away. Dogged in their goodness, they had a kind of brawn, a ruggedness that shone in their eyes and through their skin, that made them magnetic and a little bit terrifying. Or maybe it was simply because they were beautiful, talented, and rich.

And so, the conversation turned to women who couldn't have kids.

"Yes," Lena acquiesced. "The way the ad presents it is very First World, but the actual problem runs deep. Imagine if you wanted to see, to hear, to taste, but you couldn't. It's the same yearning. An elemental human desire."

Lena sported a hickey on her neck, given to her as a joke by Raj, and Elisa kept looking at its red-tinged border. She could imagine Lena, her strong arms with the blue veins popping off of them, pushing Raj away and laughing, her hair a wild, fragrant bed of hay that he collapsed into. Proximity to Lena felt invigorating, like a cosmic tailwind, as though Elisa became more beautiful, more honest, more intelligent and altruistic just by sitting next to her on the bed.

So, she told Marla it was an act of radical empathy. The longing for children elemental, like the desire for sight.

"Amazing," said Marla. "You're so young, really, to understand that." Marla folded her hands together. She had strangely stubby fingers, the nails polished clear. Was she sincere? She seemed to mean it, but how could you ever know when talking to an actress?

"I've wanted a baby for a long time," Marla said. "Zach and I both. But it's been tough. I thought it would be okay. My mom had me at forty-two. But it's not working out. I didn't picture having to go this route, but when I saw your profile I felt better about it. And now that I've actually met you, well. You're an old soul, aren't you, Elisa? Beautiful, too. A bonus."

It felt like being kissed.

The assistant came into the room, her earrings catching that bold LA light. "It's two o'clock," she said.

"Thank you so much for meeting me," Marla said. "It might sound cheesy to say it, but motherhood is the role I truly want. I just have to tell you that, Elisa. I have a feeling you already know."

Lena administered the shots twice a day, wiping Elisa's belly with alcohol swabs then plunging the needle into the spot near her belly button. Elisa swelled up. For the last few days of the medication, none of her clothing fit. Then she took a bus to Boston and they took the eggs out (Thirty-seven eggs!), put her up in a nice hotel where she slept and slept, and then she went back to school, finished her big Modernism term paper, took exams, and planned her final semester.

The money helped. She got an apartment in Harlem with two other recent grads and spent the summer applying for internships and entry-level jobs. She bought some cute interview clothes at a store with racks of delicate dresses designed by recent RISD grads. Shoes made of supple leather that molded to her feet. She procured a summer internship with a literary agent, an elderly woman who rolled her own cigarettes, ate sardines and hated all of her clients, and then in the fall, landed an entry-level assistant publicist job at one of the most esteemed publishing houses in the country. The assistants from the various departments went once a week to happy hour tapas at a bar in Union Square and Elisa would spend too much money on sangria and whatever slider or oyster everyone else ordered. And at night, she would sit on her bed, on the sheets with little lightning bolts she bought at a discount store and she would feel overwhelmed with it, that she had so easily, so simply gotten the life that she wanted.

Even the boy, Ben Rose, the friend of Raj Singh that Lena had introduced her to back in Providence, the boy she'd taken a walk with at midnight and kissed under a cherry tree so pink it looked like a party favor, tiny petals sticking to their shoes, he'd moved to Harlem, also, to start medical school at Mt. Sinai. And the two of them spent every available hour watching Fellini films, going to publishing or med school parties, and, of course, in bed.

Winter came and the city went from golden to white, and Ben asked Elisa if she'd move in with him. She hadn't seen this coming. Most of her friends went on awful date after awful date, sleeping with noncommittal boys on futons in tiny apartments, complaining about the supply and demand issue in the city (too many single women, too many men who wanted to stay single). And she felt an uncharacteristic breaking in her chest, almost like heartbreak except what followed felt like a rush. She had put her hands on his newly shaved face, his nose bumpy and honest-looking, his smell so distinct, like oil cans in the woods, and nodded.

So, that winter she spent a little more of the money on a deposit and moved her lounge chair, her mattress, her many, many books. And she and Ben set up a little home with terrariums and cinderblock bookcases to the ceiling and a little dining room table they found at consignment shop near the medical school.

Her mother would have been so proud of her. She'd always wanted to live in New York, imagined herself at museums, talking about books with sophisticated friends in outdoor bistros, trains rumbling underfoot. Sometimes, when life looked exactly like this fantasy of itself, when Elisa ate mussels with her boss at the French place on the corner and he told her she'd get a promotion, she could feel her mother in her jaw, tasting the mussels, too, and she would lose track of the conversation, imagining her mother with her pale, waxy skin, ears that stuck out too far, never quite covered up by the elaborate hair styles she favored. Her mother who would put a ghost's hand on Elisa's hand, there in these crowded places, and make the world go still.

Then, one Friday afternoon, at the store, buying things to cook for dinner, she noticed the cover of *US Weekly* on the rack.

MARLA MYLES AND ZACH GRIFTON WELCOME BABY GIRL CARSON!

She put the groceries on the conveyor belt and stared. Marla and Zach, sunglasses and perfect skin. You couldn't see the baby, burritoed up and held to Marla's chest. EXCLUSIVE PHOTOS INSIDE. She took the magazine and dropped it beside the food.

Elisa read the entire article without breathing in front of the grocery store in the freezing cold. Then, she sat down hard on a bench.

There was one picture of the baby. She had dark hair, a mild scowl, and a heart-shaped face.

She hadn't thought this far ahead, which now seemed a bald oversight. But she hadn't, because how could she? She gave Marla the gift of a baby, or had at least contributed something of herself to Marla's baby, in exchange for rent. And now this part of her would live a rarified life in Los Angeles, New York, Paris, a life she hadn't thought to imagine. Nannies and infinity pools and friends whose parents were "in the industry." Carson could have any horse her heart desired, gorgeous hand-tooled saddles, every Ariat boot.

Lena moved to Durham for medical school. Elisa didn't hear from her much anymore. "The actress had the baby," she texted. Three days later, Lena wrote back, "That's great for her." She stuck a thumb's up sign next to it.

Elisa threw away the magazine.

A year passed. Elisa tried to forget about the baby. What else could she do? She could do nothing. To think about what it meant felt like making a pledge to neurosis, like grooming her own unhappiness when actually, she had the life she wanted. Her mother would never have this life, or any life at all. But she could. And so she should.

Besides, it was only an egg. A group of cells. The same kind she tossed into New York City dumpsters every month.

The gray, damp city turned silver and green. Birds landed in trees, prancing down branches with worms and trash in their beaks. Women wore dresses without leggings or tights, their bare ankles like the start of tiny fresh twigs.

And then, in February, the publisher came to their weekly meeting. "I've got an important and exciting new partnership to announce," she said, her red hair and freckles accentuated by her bright red lipstick. "We've been chosen by Analog—the new project by Marla Myles. We'll be putting a small library of special edition, beautifully produced, classic books into every fifth-grade classroom in all five boroughs. And we need to start pitching it. Myles's team will help, of course. But be brainstorming!"

Analog. Elisa had read about it while stalking Marla online one rainy Saturday. *Get the kids off their phones. Learn to love the weight of a book.* "I know Marla," she felt like saying in the middle of the meeting. She pressed her pen deeply into her pad of paper until the nib made a black hole. She couldn't say anything. She'd signed the papers. She felt a weightless whirring, like she was both there, in the meeting, and also above it, in the sky, wrapped in the fluff of a cloud and drifting. She listened to people bat around ideas for places that might run a story, but it felt hard to hear through the cottony mist.

Back at her cubicle, Elisa stared at her screen. It made sense. The press boasted a distinguished backlist, and Marla had great taste.

She put Marla's name into the database. Amazing. Just like that. Her personal address, her brownstone in Chelsea, not her manager's, not her agent's.

Elisa went to the bathroom and sat on the toilet. She looked up the address on her phone. She stared at the street view of the brownstone, the beautiful columns, gypsy caravan windows, iron gate. The baby lived twenty minutes from this toilet.

That night, she met up with Ben at a party, but she didn't want to listen to gossip about professors or cadavers with tattoos or whatever they were talking about. She said she didn't feel well.

Outside, a woman and a little girl crouched on a stoop, trying to make a bed out of a ripped child's sleeping bag and some dirty blankets.

"Hey." The woman had a low, confident voice and a big scab on her scalp where the hair no longer grew. Elisa felt herself recoil, but she made herself stand there, she made herself look the woman in the face. The little girl stared at Elisa with open, curious eyes. She had braided pigtails with big, glittering butterfly hairbands.

"Can you help us out?" the woman said. Elisa had half a sandwich in her purse. She pulled it out and looked at it. Then she took out her wallet and gave the woman two hundred dollars. Because she had it. Because her first reaction had been to flee. The woman stared at the money then quickly put it into her shirt.

There had been only one day between the accident and her mother's death, a coma and then organ failure. She'd been a senior in high school, already admitted to the college of her dreams, focused on the beckoning future. And then she became a child in a hospital, screaming for her mother to hear her as her mother's hand, warm in hers, did not grab back. She tried and she tried and she tried. For days, for weeks after all the machines were turned off, after they'd rolled the corpse away to the funeral home, after her mother's sister Serena had come and held Elisa in her arms and wept into her hair, she couldn't get her hands to stop doing it, grabbing and grabbing and grabbing.

Once an egg, then a fetus in a womb, then a baby in her mother's arms, then an orphan, she now stood on a dark street in a large city, a bunch of people clustering in front of a Starbuck's. And somewhere, her baby existed, too. She couldn't touch her mother. She couldn't touch her baby.

Mom, she typed into the "To" line of her messages when she got to her door. The word just stared at her.

She walked by the brownstone several times a week, adding a good mile to her work commute. She wasn't stalking. She felt curious. Could she catch a glimpse of them, this family she'd enabled? If she just said hello, maybe she could pop this bubble that she now lived within. Maybe Marla would smile at her, hug her, invite her over to their house where they'd eat chicken skewers and laugh as the baby tried to prize meat from the stick. Lovely and pure and communal, a real modern family. She'd bring Ben over and he'd understand, both the reason she'd donated and why she kept it secret. Everything would normalize—be better than normal. Forward-thinking and compassionate, exactly as it should be.

She never saw anyone. She tried going a little earlier, and every time she rounded the corner her heart went crazy, her hands itched. Almost mystical, the way the subway car released the workers into the new light, the city filled with cheeping birds, the clean feel of the spring morning air as the sun rose and rose and rose. The bustle of early shifts. The walking of fussy babies by tired women holding metal coffee cups. None of them Marla.

She'd all but given up. Then, in June, she spotted her. Marla in a large gray wool coat, scarf, sunglasses, and glamorous turban thing, carrying a little dark-haired child in a bright blue jacket. A car waited for Marla in front. Twenty yards from the brownstone, Elisa had a minute, one minute to yell out before Marla made her way to the car.

Then Marla turned toward her, scanning the sidewalk like she'd been expecting Elisa to walk down it. Elisa froze under a well-pruned tree. She was the thrum of a harp chord, the reverberation of a drum, not a girl, but the need of a girl, noise, anticipation. The space between her and Marla filled with summersaulting balls of light. But Marla turned back toward the car. She lifted Carson to her face and kissed her before handing her to a young man who buckled the toddler into the car seat.

Her voice felt frozen. No. The world dropped this moment into her hands so that she wouldn't have to strain to catch it.

"Marla!" Elisa said, raspy, like she had woodchips in her throat and Marla turned again. She narrowed her eyes and pushed the pretty turban off her forehead. Then she said something to the young man who leaned in to hear her as she got in beside the baby. The car took off.

Why was she crying? What had she expected would happen? That Marla would be excited to see her? Delusional. She probably said she wouldn't do something like this in one of the billion papers she'd signed.

The heat of August settled over the city, and she and Ben took a trip out to his parent's cabin in Tahoe. There, by a fire under a full moon, he took out a bag of trail mix and poured the contents into his hand. From it, he extracted his grandmother's engagement ring, a large diamond in a flower setting.

Ben knew nothing, but he couldn't help it. He'd been a little baby in a warm and loving family, nursed from the breast of a friendly, intelligent mother, grew up with no real heartache, excelled in school, gone straight to medical school. He knew work and reward, work and reward, nothing complicated, nothing tragic. He was a spiritual virgin and a piece of her floated away from him that night, or had been floating for a while, but she said yes, as she always knew she would, if he asked.

"I definitely want kids," Ben said to her early in their courtship, lying in bed in that first apartment she'd rented with the egg money, under those lightning bolt sheets. She'd curled her toes around his toes, felt their hairy separation. His body lean and long, the warmth of the morning—sun through the slightly open window, smell of car exhaust and cement and cooking oil from the falafel place underneath them.

"Yeah," Elisa had said. "At some point." She ran her hands up his chest and then turned over—too abruptly, probably.

"What?" he said. "Do you not want kids?"

"I do," she said. "Do you want coffee?"

"Do you see yourself with boy babies or girl babies?" he asked her, and she went into the kitchen to make food.

That had been the extent of it. Still in their early twenties, they had decades to figure it out. She wanted to edit books. To have an office with floor to ceiling bookcases, a vase of fresh flowers near a wall of thank you notes from famous authors. She wanted conversations at restaurants that made her blood course faster, that gave her brain the spins. She wanted to be at the edge of things, to feel the feeling a book gave to you when it did something new and lively, when it bent the cultural conversation away from its expected course, charging the air. This future pulled at her. She wanted to use her restless mind. It had a clock of its own. *What does it mean to be "maternal?"* she wrote in her journal. *Is it actually simply the desire to create? Or to be part of creation? To nurture something into being? Does it have to be a baby?*

Part of her wanted to tell him what she'd done, but she'd signed a lot of forms, and also, she sensed she shouldn't. For some other, hard to pinpoint reason. She sensed it might complicate something later, down the road.

They found the wedding dress, white satin with complex white embroidery along the bodice and sleeves, in a bag with purses and wallets, packed carefully in a plastic storage bag with cedar bars. It felt so important to find this dress after Serena told her it existed. But now that she saw it, she knew she'd never wear it.

"It would feel like drag. I think I just want to wear a regular dress," she said to Ben. "Just something pretty. Something with color. And great shoes. I don't know." She folded the dress back up.

"Hey, look," Ben said. He'd opened a large storage box and pulled out a small white sweater with little raspberry pockets. Elisa knelt over the box as Ben pulled things from it. Tiny leather booties. A white dress with a scalloped collar. A blue polyester crocheted sweater that Elisa remembered. It had been her mother's as a child, and then Elisa's, knit by a grandmother she never knew.

"She saved this stuff for your kids," Ben said. Then he grinned at her and made to embrace her, to kiss her. To make the baby there, amidst boxes in the little cramped unit. She grabbed the blue sweater. And then a few of the other baby things. She crammed them in her bag. She shoved the wedding dress back in the box.

"Let's just go," she said.

Her mother loved being a mother and so Elisa never really thought about it, her natural maternal gifts. She'd just been there in her life, a fixture, as plain as grass or sidewalks. She had been in the foreground, then in the background, but always a cord that Elisa could reach back and feel. Then the cord snapped. A world without grass or sidewalks, a world where suddenly you had to tromp around on sodden, uneven earth, wobbling and buckling with no one to catch you if you fell.

"I could watch you all day," her mother used to say to her, her voice nearly a purr. "My sweet Elisa, my girl."

Her mother would have pulled those baby clothes out of storage. "My baby's having a baby . . ." Elisa could almost hear it, the voice of her mother, the cringing sweetness that would make Elisa pull away despite how much part of her wanted to cover herself in it, that cloying love. Leave me be and never leave me. She reached in her bag and stuck her hand into the scratchy blue fibers of the sweater.

Sex with Ben was fine. Solid sex, Lena would have called it. Lena didn't talk that much about sex, but Elisa inferred, from the stray clues, that it involved certain cultivated pleasures imagined by women more worldy than Elisa. She loved Ben for his kindness, so much kinder than the boyfriend who handed her Sani-Wipes before going down on her, watching her wipe with disgust on his face. Or the many who simply didn't text back, pretended not to see her as they chatted up another woman at a party.

She and Ben kissed and fondled. Sometimes it even got messy and angular, a body hard against a wall, hair clutched in a fist. But mostly it felt pleasant, like a warm bath.

And during sex that night, as Ben rocked on top of her, she imagined his sperm cascading out, unleashed and free, racing through her cervix, up fallopian tubes to find her egg. Her fresh, Ivy League egg. "You are an old soul," Marla said. With young eggs, she now thought. What kind of baby would they make, she and Ben? She already knew what kind of baby she would make with Zach Grifton. A dark-haired beauty with her own eyes, with Zach's heart-shaped face.

It was nothing. A donation. Like donating a kidney. You made life with your life. You gave a gift. You opened your heart and you mothered the world. You mothered the world, said Lena, before she left and discarded her old friends, so busy now with med school and maybe with Raj, who knew.

"You mothered the world," said Lena, who had not, herself, donated eggs. Who had not donated anything, as far as Elisa could remember. Even that red dress she'd loaned Elisa had to be dry-cleaned and returned.

Ben groaned, unleashing millions of sperm, each one of them a possible baby, a legion of babies that would never be because she took a pill. All those pointless, doomed Ivy League sperm

"What's up?" he said, sweat glistening on his brow. "Did you come? Do you want me to do something else?"

"No," she said, pulling him to her. The will to pull him so close and to send him away.

She showed the ring to her friends at work. Her boss bought her cupcakes and Ben's mother sent flowers. His sister started calling Elisa about the wedding, and the two of them went over and over venues, making elaborate lists of pros and cons. They'd get married in Tahoe, but have a big party in New York, too.

She found herself swept into the chatter of Ben's big family, happily absorbed in their little mini-dramas. An alcoholic aunt who wanted to be Elisa's matron of honor. Ben's brother's claim that the date interfered with his bike trip to Italy. The chatter of that big family a happy, annoying blanket she could pull over herself.

Marla and Zach wanted a closed donation, no way for the child to find her even as an adult. At the time, Elisa didn't care. Now she understood they'd probably never tell the child about her, about the egg. They didn't need to. They could buy houses and horses and probably parts of the sea. They could buy children with great cellular CVs.

They needed so little. Why had it been her business to help them?

Carson looked, in the newest US Weekly photos, a lot like Elisa had as a toddler. That same pert expression. The same curls against the nape of her neck. She came from Elisa, would always be part of her, a lost part. At times, this filled Elisa with a haunted but satisfying pang. From her body, a seed, a girl, a family. Other times, it made her a little ill.

The wedding occurred in August. Elisa's friends from work came in their consignment designer dresses and plastic-framed glasses. She kissed Ben as two birds fought in a tree above them, and everyone pretended not to see it, the feathers drifting down and landing on Elisa's royal blue dress.

A year passed. Elisa moved to editorial, assisting another young editor with her fiction list. And then another year passed, and Ben finished med school. And Elisa stopped taking the pill and soon, a little white stick told them they were expecting. An Ivy League egg and Ivy League sperm. The baby would be a genius.

She could feel the tug of it, something leading invisibly forward, to a future she couldn't imagine, into the arms of her mother again in some strange, ghostly-yet-totally-visceral way. The baby inside of her pressing her skin to her jeans and making her weep at videos of heroic dogs. Soon, she'd be swept into it, what it really meant to mother—not the world, but one specific, squirming infant.

In line, buying cinnamon rolls, she saw a photo of Marla on the cover of *Glamour*. "Modern Mothering with Marla," the magazine promised. She picked it up and outside that same grocery store that she'd cried outside of three years earlier, she cried again. Carson wore a short furry white coat and bizarre little boots. But that wasn't the thing that struck her. No. Marla was pregnant, too. Probably with another of Elisa's eggs.

You could make a person, but you could not always stay with the person that you made. Nothing in the female mind could make sense of that. But nevertheless, the truth sat there on top of Elisa like a turd.

Ben was visiting his brother for the weekend, and so Elisa had the apartment to herself. She went to the closet and pulled out the brown sack in which she'd put the clothes from her childhood. The little blue sweater, made by a grandmother she never knew, worn by a mother who died too young, then worn by her before she had any concept of loss. She carefully wrapped it in beautiful paper, then set it in a box and penned the address. *For Carson*, she wrote. *My first.*

THE
FLOWER

In the dream, Gretta traveled back to her first day of college, the day she met Adam in the dining hall. She listened to him go on about political strife in South Africa, but then at the moment she would've started walking with him, back to his dorm, the dream paused and the choice seemed to float before her and she woke up to the noise of the garbage trucks. She stared at the weak, early light through her window and felt the feeling that had plagued her since the quarantine started: that she wasn't alone in her room.

She looked at the small jars of water lined up on the coffee table in front of the windows, marked with Sharpie so she'd know how much water had been consumed in the night. The glasses were still basically full. But a flower lay next to the table, on the floor. A daffodil.

The daffodil curled into a c-shape and raised its yellow head. It nodded. Then it laid back down straight.

She rolled over.

"Gretta," said the flower. "Please shut the windows. There's quite a breeze!"

Gretta shut her eyes and tried to be back inside of her dream. She forced herself there, kids milling about under a big outdoor tent on a grassy lawn. Adam talking and talking, his dark eyes very alert, his brain so lively you could almost hear it working, a rushing river, a far-off aircraft, and she had her tray of food.

"Fine," said the flower. Gretta opened her eyes and turned slowly back to watch the flower raise itself, using its petals as arms, then shimmy up the leg of the table. It came to a rest in front of the open window.

Gretta got out of bed, the terrible feeling in her body almost like a roommate at this point. The feeling came with her to the bathroom where she sat on the toilet and cried for a minute. But crying felt ridiculous in all this isolation. She could toss the flower out the window. But tomorrow it would just be something else. So, she went back to the bedroom, picked up the flower and brought it with her into the kitchen.

"Would you like anything?" she asked it. "Breakfast?"

"You're a love," said the flower. "Just water with a little sugar is good."

Gretta got out a glass and filled it, sprinkled the requested sugar and placed the flower inside.

"Very nice," said the flower.

She made herself oatmeal, as she'd run out of eggs.

The flower sighed and began to move its yellow corona in small yogic bends. Gretta watched it for a while, spooning oatmeal into her mouth.

"How shall we spend the day?" asked the flower.

"It's a quarantine," said Gretta.

"I'm not living under a rock," said the flower. "Of course, it's a quarantine. But the day has arrived, has it not?"

"The day has arrived," said Gretta.

Gretta got up to wash her dishes. "We could watch movies," she said. "Or sort tax documents. Or read. Or do a puzzle."

"Maybe we could talk," the flower said.

At the sink, she heard the clink and slosh of the glass falling over. She made no move to clean it up. She went back to her bedroom.

Again, the jars in the light of the morning. One jar did have a large amount of water missing now. She lay down, pulled the blankets up over her head. She moved her legs so that they created a tent, so that her low back lay flat, and she tried to breathe deep and slow. On her nightstand, a ladybug sauntered towards her.

"For fuck's sake," Gretta said. The ladybug didn't say anything. It froze where it was. Then it turned and crawled to the wall and vanished from her sight.

This was no way to live, trapped in the box of an apartment for the third month in a row. It wasn't even a very nice apartment. She'd barely spent any time here, before the quarantine. She kept herself busy. She worked every shift she could work. She went out with her friends from the restaurant. She took an Italian class, yoga classes. Now, she stared at the barren walls. For a month, she had exercised alongside a woman on her laptop, engaging her buttocks and thighs, breathing deep, etcetera. Then she had braved the outdoors and tried to jog, feeling the heft and jiggle of her un-jogged body so distinctly, it began to give her a complex. Mercifully, she twisted her ankle so she stopped. She'd talked on the phone, had Zoom dates with friends, all the things everyone did. She filed for unemployment and it didn't go through, so she refiled for unemployment until it did. And then a woman in her building came down with the virus and died, and the super asked them all to stay inside their units while women in hazmat suits sanitized the common areas. Just a few hours of hazmat women, but a fear of leaving set in.

She lay on the bed, waiting. The water had been drunk by somebody.

Gretta, said the wall.

No, said Gretta.

The wall wasn't speaking, probably. But the issue of the drunk water remained. There was the issue of the virus and of course, of Adam, and when she thought about it, the voice of the flower reminded her of someone she couldn't place—a particular inflection, a weird way of sounding both prim and egoistical.

She got back up. She took the three glasses to the bathroom and dumped the water out. What did it matter, her little science projects?

She got into the shower, the water so hot it hurt. She watched it turn her skin red. She studied her arms. They were just her arms, covered in freckles, leading to her knobby wrists and then her hands. Her mother had had beautiful hands, hands she bragged about, and it made an impression on Gretta. For a long stretch around thirteen, she felt ashamed of her stubby hands, the fingernails like fat little shovels. Now she balled them into fists.

She went back into the bedroom, put on a bra, underwear, pants. She stared at the T-shirt drawer, then opted for a dress from her closet instead.

She paused to see if any of her clothes would say anything, but it was just a morning, just clothing, just her little cramped closet, smelling vaguely of shoe sweat. It wasn't glamorous, her life. Her mother had wanted her to have a glamorous life, had encouraged her to move to this city where she could spread her wings, but all she had managed to do was spread tablecloths on the lovely little tables at Le Petit Oiseau.

Her phone rang. It was Anastasia.

"Hi," said Gretta.

"Heya," said her sister. "How are you holding up?"

Anastasia had just had a second baby when the quarantine started five months ago. Last week, when Anastasia called, she kept whizzing a little blender thing, making coconut squash for Sasha. She texted Gretta photos every day. Sasha with his sister Louise on the big, grassy lawn of their Oregon house. Sasha holding a giant sunflower. Sasha eating coconut squash, the orange stuff all over his face.

"I'm okay," Gretta said, sitting up. Across the room, a photo of her sister at age six, her buck-teeth, her huge green eyes.

"Did I wake you up?"

"No," said Gretta. "I just got up, but I wasn't actually sleeping."

"Sounds glorious," said Anastasia. The baby made a sound. Gretta heard a rustle and a bunch of talking, scolding of Louise. Then Anastasia said, "Anything new?"

Gretta turned over to face the card table and stared at the slats of light coming through her blinds. Now, fully morning, the sun seemed oblivious to everything, just shining its light on the fucked-up planet.

"Nothing to report," Gretta said.

"I actually have a favor to ask," Anastasia said. "Remember those dresses you put aside for me when you lost that weight? Could you mail them to me? I don't fit into anything here, and I can't go shop, and I can't be bothered with online returns and stuff."

Gretta had forgotten all about the dresses. "I'll have to look for them."

"I hate to make you go to the post office," said Anastasia. "But maybe it's good to get out. Just be careful. Here's Louise," said Anastasia, and soon

Gretta was chatting with her three-year-old niece about ice cream flavors and the room was just her room again, the morning light just light.

She went into her closet, but couldn't find the dresses. She made her way back to the kitchen.

"I could use a little help here," said the flower. She went into the laundry alcove to rummage through the cabinets in there.

"Is there a reason you don't want to help me?" said the flower.

She might've put them in the storage unit, in which case, she'd need to leave the apartment, get on her Vespa, drive to the unit, touch a lot of surfaces and then drive back, none of which felt surmountable. Though, it might be good to leave the apartment.

She stood up and grabbed her keys.

"Gretta," said the flower. Gretta looked at the flower, pathetic in a puddle on the table. She grabbed the flower, too, and left the apartment.

The Vespa leapt to life beneath her. It sent its energy right into her body and Gretta felt her hair in the breeze, her shoulders straightening. The warm air circled her. It even seemed to love her. She tried to love it back. She put on her magenta helmet, the flower clutched in her fist along with the handle. The flower gasped and laughed as they pulled onto the street, zoomed down it to the corner where she took the entrance ramp onto the thoroughfare toward the industrial part of the city, where she'd rented the small unit for Adam's things. Number 161—just a cheap metal affair with a red door that slid up.

The world, here it was, as if nothing had happened. The sun made the mica in the concrete jump and dance. Spots of rust dotted the red sliding doors. Inside, all the boxes. BOOKS, RANDOM, PAPERS, PHOTOS. A moving company packed Adam's things more than a year ago and brought them out here. She walked the small path through the boxes.

"Gretta," said the flower. Gretta looked down at it, wilted now, tattered from the ride. "Should you be here? Is this where you should be right now?"

"Who are you?" Gretta asked the flower.

Gretta put the flower down on a low box and began to look for other boxes, boxes from her bedroom. She sort of recalled shoving some of her own things in boxes during that sodden and bleary time.

"Have you spoken with him?" the flower asked.

"Who?" said Gretta.

"Who," scoffed the flower.

Gretta looked at the flower. She could throw it out of the unit.

"I would advise against it," said the flower. Gretta went back to looking at the boxes. There were a few, way up at the top, that looked familiar, old banker's boxes. She needed some kind of ladder. She piled a few plastic boxes, climbed them, and managed to topple the top box into her hands. Her first try, and the dresses revealed themselves: purple cotton with flowers, deep green velour with maroon piping. She started to load them into her backpack. She could just go straight to the post office from here and it would be done, a task accomplished. Human hands would carry her dresses to a truck where they'd be driven through wilderness and towns and eventually be sorted in Portland—and the flower yelped.

One of the boxes moved. Gretta backed up and the moment she did, the cheery, rusted red door slammed down and Adam climbed out of the box.

She reached for a box to steady herself and took a deep breath. Then she held the dress she'd been holding—the green one—and covered her face with it.

"I had an idea for the xenophobia chapter," said Adam. "I think the main issue with it was that I didn't order it well. It should have started with diamonds."

"Adam?" She didn't remove the dress from her face.

"Did you read it?" he asked. "Just wondering if you agree."

"Adam?"

"What?" he said. And then she began to cry into the dress. What was happening? She didn't want to wreck the dress with mascara, but she hadn't worn mascara in months, it was a quarantine. Would he come forward and hold her? She missed him so much.

She lowered the dress. Adam stood there, looking slightly concerned and slightly annoyed. The South Africa book he'd been working on was in that box: UNFINISHED MANUSCRIPT. Then there was a loud POP, and she saw the bits of brain on the boxes behind him and she screamed, and as she screamed, the brain turned to lavender feathers and Adam became flat and white like a paper doll and disappeared.

She ran toward the red door, shoved it open, lurched outside and threw up.

"You weren't prepared for that," said the flower.

"Fuck you," said Gretta. "Go away. Leave me alone."

"You're angry now," said the flower. Gretta stood outside, heaving. No one walked by. Probably no one had been here for months. Why would you come here in a quarantine? What could you possibly need? She yearned for a crowd. A normal fucking inhabited world.

Above her the sun. Below her the cement. A crow landed on the chain link fence and cawed. It turned and looked at Gretta.

"You should put words to it," said the flower.

It clicked. That voice.

The year Adam had the job in Indianapolis, teaching a special seminar in African history, she'd missed her friends, felt distant from Adam who was in one of his frenzies, writing a book, teaching, attending endless meetings. Maybe you should see a therapist, said Anastasia, so she'd Googled therapists and landed on this woman. She couldn't remember her name anymore. The psychotherapist had a degree from somewhere fancy and wore no make-up or jewelry, just expensive, dark sweaters and leather slip-ons. Gretta sat in a chair in the dim office and tried to talk about her loneliness, but somehow the topic of suicide came up—not her own wish for it—she'd never felt that way. She must've been talking about Eliza, her friend who made grim indie films about self-immolation. And the therapist gazed out the window said, "The suicidal seem more willing to face a truth that most of us can't, or won't. I think they're very brave."

Gretta stared at the therapist who looked vaguely at the parking lot out the window. What the fuck, she said to Anastasia.

Gretta never went back. The therapist never called her about her missed appointments, never billed her. That therapist had had this voice, nasal, ponderous, egotistical.

"If you verbalize your feelings, they lose their power over you," said the flower.

"I feel like I need a toothbrush," said Gretta, spitting.

"You don't always need to be clever," said the flower. "Do you feel like you need to be clever with me?"

Gretta went into the unit and grabbed her backpack. She shut the red door. She locked it.

"Gretta!" the flower called from inside the unit. "GRETTA!"

As soon as it was possible to do such a thing, she'd hire a moving service to bring all the boxes to The Salvation Army. Or she'd pay to have them all shipped to Adam's mother. She wouldn't return to this place ever again.

You're dead to me! She thought. Ha.

The Vespa wouldn't start. She'd run out of gas. She hadn't been paying attention.

The sky looked ominous now, the air muggy. Clouds rolled over themselves in a hurry to clog the sky.

She could call a ride service. But she hadn't worn a mask. She took out her phone to scroll through her friends, but her phone was also dead, which seemed impossible, as she'd just charged it. She pressed it and pressed and it and pressed it. A drop of rain fell on the screen, followed by more and more drops.

She unlocked the red door. The fucking flower lay where she'd put it, on a low box. She waited, but the flower said nothing. Gretta looked at the box labeled UNFINISHED MANUSCRIPT. It was still open. She could see the papers in there, Adam's boxy penmanship in the margins. She reached in and took out a stack. Indeed, his xenophobia chapter. She didn't feel like reading it. She took all of the papers of out of the box. At the bottom, lay a key. She picked it up. It didn't look like a house key, more like a key to antique box, three little arches at the top, one tooth at the base. She didn't recall packing an antique box, but then again, she'd had help packing.

"You wish you had a key," said the flower.

"I do have a key," said Gretta.

"You wish you could unlock the past," said the flower.

"I wish you would just be a flower," said Gretta. "I wish things would go back to normal. I want to wake up in the morning and get dressed and go to the restaurant."

"I'm not a genie," said the flower.

"You wanted to know how I felt," said Gretta. "Where is Adam?"

"Where is Adam?" asked the flower.

"Is Adam with you?"

"Where is Adam," said the flower, as if it were some kind of profound thing, as if they should consider it from many angles.

"Did you kill yourself, too?" asked Gretta.

"Do you feel you need to know this about me? Do you feel it would benefit our work together?"

"We aren't working together," Gretta said.

"We are," said the flower. "That is what we're doing."

"We aren't," said Gretta. "You're a flower."

"I'm a flower," said the flower. "Like you are a woman."

"Is that a riddle?"

"Do you want it to be a riddle?"

Gretta sighed. She looked around the storage unit. "It doesn't matter," she said.

"Nothing else matters," said the flower.

"What am I going to do?" said Gretta.

"What *are* you going to do?" said the flower. "You were not prepared for this."

Gretta turned and opened a box. Inside, Adam's old CDs. Why had she stored these? She looked at them—Smokey Robinson, The Ramones, even an old Bette Midler. Like everything else, the collection made no sense. Adam used to put on "Wind Beneath My Wings" sometimes during breakfast, when he was very upbeat and he'd shout along with the words and twirl her around, make her cappuccino with his fancy machine that was probably in a box in here someplace. She tossed the CDs back and opened another box. Old family silverware that his mother had given him. Beneath the silverware, some old books. She opened another one—sweaters, several she'd knit for him. She pulled one out, blue argyle. She tossed it into a corner. The next box held his bathroom supplies. What the hell. Who'd packed these? Shaving cream, plastic razors. The razors still had hair sticking to them—still had wettish shaving cream—

She dropped the bathroom supplies and closed the box. Was someone living in here? It hadn't really been Adam—just her quarantined, grief-addled mind—right?

"You think that the rational mind is the answer to the world, don't you?" asked the flower.

"I have really had enough," said Gretta. "I mean it."

"You think your mind holds the key."

"My hands are holding the key," said Gretta.

"Interesting," said the flower, as if Gretta had just said something truly remarkable. "Your hands."

Gretta put the key in her pocket. It actually looked like a key from her grandmother's key collection. It likely unlocked a box long destroyed.

Too bad she didn't find gasoline in the unit. She'd fill her Vespa and torch the place.

She took the box with the razors and put it outside. She looked again, all the boxes stacked, containing things she never wanted to see again, and then she saw a box that she swore hadn't been there moments before. A lacquered black box, the size of a small traveling trunk, wedged in the corner. She unearthed it, and indeed, the antique key fit. She lifted the lid, and in it, gasoline in a delicate looking long-nosed pouring vessel and a lighter. She ran out to the Vespa, poured the gasoline in. The bike started up. Womb-womb, said the bike.

She ran back into the unit with the vessel, just a little gas left at the bottom. Should she do it? She looked at the lavender feathers. She looked at the flower. She could feel the flower there, a silent tension.

"You're after the wrong kind of catharsis," said the flower. "I hoped you'd come to that understanding through our work together, but I see I must intervene."

Gretta walked over to the box with the flower on it and poured the gasoline there.

"What good do you think this will do?" said the flower.

Gretta watched the flame of the lighter, the blue giving way to clear and then orange.

"It won't do anything," said the flower. "You're wasting your energy."

She lowered the lighter and almost burned her hand as the blaze blasted to life. She backed out of the unit, something like laughter coming through her body.

She ran back to her Vespa. Now, the dark clouds moved off the blue, a sparkling expanse of world before her. The sun made the wet road smell like rocks. She was an alive little thing, her hair out behind her, her stubby hands gripping the handles of her bike. She lived, what a trip. Bones covered with skin, a spirit she couldn't explain. She was probably also a felon, a sloppy felon with a crime very easy to trace.

She parked the Vespa and went inside. Her phone worked. How crazy. She snapped a photo of the dresses for her sister.

She wiped up the spilled water from the table. Anastasia would be excited to have the dresses, especially the green one she so envied. As soon as the package arrived, she'd put it on and be unable to look in the mirror, her children, hanging off her like monkeys. The dress would have a second life. It would go to the store, go on picnics, fight with Lukas, get peanut butter on its shoulder. Should it feel comforting?

Her phone rang. She let it go to voicemail, then checked the message. It was the manager of the storage unit calling to tell her that her door had been left open, some boxes gone through. Could she call him back right away?

You couldn't live like this, all alone in a box in a building on a random piece of land in the middle of a continent. It wasn't really life. Time stretched itself in psychedelic orbs, but it didn't move the way it should. Adam hadn't known a special truth. No special truth existed.

The week before he'd done it, they went to a costume party. He dressed as a purple bird with this huge lavender boa and she went as his worm in a pink sleeping bag. And in the kitchen at that party, he told stories about their trip to Mexico City the previous fall, and he'd made the whole room laugh, made Gretta laugh so hard she cried. She tried to wipe her eyes with the boa and purple feathers came off which had seemed even funnier. After the party, in bed, they went over the part of the Mexico story where Gretta fell into a hole, not even that funny, and they'd laughed more, and Adam turned to her in bed, his beautiful, open face in the lamplight, those wide, dark eyes of his that startled her, even a decade into a marriage, and he said, "Gretta, you are my whole heart." He said things like this all the time. And he meant them. And now it made her feel like a golf ball had wedged itself in her throat and she couldn't breathe.

When Adam went to their old building's laundry area to shoot himself through the head, he left daffodils on the table for her.

She folded the dresses. She removed the key from her pocket. She waited for a voice to bother her, for the silence to talk again. After a while, she went down the stairs to the sidewalk. She surveyed the flower beds in front of her building, slightly unkempt, messy with blooms. "Beautiful weather," a woman said, walking past. Gretta watched her disappear around the corner with her prancing little dog.

Gretta stepped over the small fake fence. A few masked joggers glanced at her. She picked all of the flowers, even the daffodils.

She set the flowers in a vase by the brightest kitchen window. Their petals caught the sunlight, pinned it to themselves greedily. If they spoke, she couldn't hear them. She moved her fingers over their speechless parts. Here we are, they said with their silken petals, fragile filaments, and surprisingly tough stems. What a trip.

A GUN IN
THE FIRST ACT

"If in the first act you have hung a pistol on the wall,
then in the following one it should be fired.
Otherwise, don't put it there."

CHEKHOV

I'd say I'm losing them, but I fear I never had them. The bearded one keeps looking down at his notebook, fussing with a rainbow-colored paper clip. He slips the paper clip off the paper, lets it clamp around his fingers. Then he puts it back. He carefully bends it out of shape and then back into shape. Too close together, his features dance around the maypole of his nose. Even his ears reach forward, as if trying to clutch his cheeks. His facial hair grows thick and high so that only a goggle-like section of skin remains visible.

There are three men in the hotel room besides me, the female candidate. They sit in a semicircle in front of a large white bed. Short on chairs, they offered me the upholstered bench where you might drape a nightie. The one with the beard is the chair of the search committee, Professor Raphael McDougal. The one with the beige orthopedic shoes is Professor John Dutton. The third, Professor Jerry Burns, with his graying ponytail and John Lennon glasses, might be described as an aging hippie if his eyes weren't full of sharp, ruthless hatred and his lip didn't keep twisting derisively off to the side. Burns has been making this face at me since he opened the door. Clearly, he didn't want to invite me here.

"So, Imani," says beige-shoed Professor Dutton. He asks me a question about fundraising.

"I know it's unusual to find an academic who's good at raising money," I say. "But I did a lot of it for Baner College when they started having financial trouble. I'm good at a fancy dinner. And really, I'd be more than happy to do whatever's necessary."

Professor Jerry Burns folds himself forward, a raptor getting ready to take off, and grabs for a Dixie cup of water on a small stool—my water, incidentally.

"You are so very willing," he says dryly.

John Dutton ignores Burns. He's already onto his next question, written in tidy penmanship on a steno pad, yellow with age: How do I do as a team player? Can I cite some recent collaborations?

John Dutton raises his brow anticipatorily, but I can see McDougal isn't listening. He has that paper clip almost all the way dismantled, and slowly, with focus, begins to twist it back into form the opposite way of its natural curves. He does this with such tenderness, smoothing the small metal bar with his index finger, nudging it along. He's like a mother sheep prodding a newborn lamb.

"Oh, sorry," he says, when he sees all six of our eyes on the rainbow clip. He holds it for a moment, and it looks like he might toss it in the waste bin. But instead he lifts one hip up out of his chair and puts the clip in his pocket, patting it lightly. His eyes look incredibly glassy and bloodshot.

I answer the team player question. I worked at Baner College, a tiny liberal arts college outside of San Francisco, until it gambled badly on a set of bonds to cure its debt. Before the college folded, when the small faculty thought we might be able to save it and our incomes, I spent days and nights writing letters, hosting fundraising dinners, calling alumni. All this, of course, in addition to teaching full-time, advising freshman, and serving on committees. We worked together, tirelessly.

I see Burns roll his eyes. "The perfect candidate," he says. "But I wonder, did you go the extra mile, Imani? While you were busy martyring yourself, did you donate any organs to this fatally ill school?" He crumples the Dixie cup into a wad and leaves it, forlorn and ruined, on the stool.

John Dutton smiles at me as if we've just noted the fine day outside. I look at Burns, lip pulled down, then back at John Dutton's friendly, watery smile.

I fight the flicker of indignation, the desire to face Burns and ask him why he invited me here, had me fly from Portland to Denver, waste my thousand dollars on a flight, a room, and Banana Republic suit, if he was only going to ridicule me from his stupid wooden chair. But I know that if I say anything, the story will turn on me. These academics will go down to the bar and talk about that lunatic short story writer, Imani Roberts, her lack of restraint, her impulsivity, her stridency. And though the other faculty won't care all that much, this information will live in the backs of their minds like a bad smell in a restaurant. They'll move on with their lives, but when I apply for jobs, for grants or publications, they won't know why they do it, but they'll push me aside.

"Excuse me," McDougal says, standing. The bathroom juts off the entryway. We all hear the fan go on. Then a long, vital-sounding stream of urine hits the toilet water. No one speaks. Finally, it stops. John Dutton clears his throat. And then it starts again, a tiny, tinkling echo. Then it stops for good, and McDougal appears in the doorway, rubbing his nose. The quiet where the flush should be feels loud and large.

Interviews for academic jobs in this field always take place in hotel rooms at the annual AWP conference. It saves the universities money to have all the candidates fly out to these phony conventions where midlist writers improvise about faux-academic topics while battling their hangovers. It's horrible and compromising. But it doesn't matter, because this is how it's done, and there are enough of us clamoring for jobs that it's simple supply and demand. If the rules are buy a nicer than average suit, fly yourself across the nation, put yourself up, and arrive at a bedroom door at a quarter to nine smiling and saying *yes, of course, I will do anything you want*, then you just do it.

"Well," John Dutton says. "Excuse that. We've been doing back-to-back interviews all morning." He seems to realize this won't comfort me, and sets his pen down. "Congratulations, by the way. We had six-hundred and seventy-four applicants, and we're down to twenty now."

John Dutton seems like a nice man: a gentle if ineffective father. I would have been happy with a father like him, if I'd had one at all. I imagine him with a crepey-faced wife, her white hair like a dandelion puff, serving out hearty meals of beef and carrots. Ancient paperbacks would line wooden bookcases in his living room, his bathroom, his bedroom, his hall. John Dutton asks me about my scholarship.

I open my mouth to answer, but McDougal stops at the minibar. He crouches in front of it and cracks his knuckles. He shuffles some stuff around. With his unwashed hands, he opens a string cheese noisily and bites into it.

"Raphael," says John Dutton. McDougal looks at him with his deeply bloodshot eyes. His pupils don't look quite right. They're too big. He slowly peels a line of cheese off the stick.

"Yeah?" he asks.

John Dutton gestures to me with his head.

There's a weird sound coming from the hotel, a burst of an alarm that quickly goes quiet. It seems to startle McDougal out his stupor, momentarily.

"Oh, sorry, sorry. Do you want anything?" he asks me. "We have cheese, chocolate milk, and Red Bull."

A friend advised me not to have caffeine before an interview, so all morning my head has felt stuffed with cotton. I would dearly love a Red Bull. McDougal can see it in the guilty way I look at the can. He hands me one. I pretend to set it in my lap, and with the smallest movements of my fingers, I wipe it off on my shirt.

"Give me one of those," Burns says. He opens one and guzzles it like it's a Gatorade.

I Googled these men before this interview. Every candidate did, I'm sure. McDougal has the most literary credibility. He's written two books of highly stylized short stories that everyone pretends to love, though what they really love are his drug-addled bouts of mania. Rumor has it that at a party, he took off all his clothes and asked Don DeLillo to put his hands on his bare flesh. Don DeLillo left the party, and McDougal wept. Another time, while in Chicago to give a reading, he had the grad student driving him pull over at a car lot where he bought a Jeep Cherokee on a whim because, he told her, F. Scott Fitzgerald once did the same. One might expect that erratic behavior like this might threaten a job at a public university, but his tenure appears bulletproof.

Nothing sordid or curious follows beige-clad John Dutton. He's your run of the mill English scholar, anemic and fine-boned. All I could find about him, besides academic papers, were a few links to professor review websites in which his "hotness ratings" were predictably low.

Burns, though, has the unluckiest online presence. In 1986, his novel, *A Boy with Wax Wings*, came out with a large New York publishing house, and the *New York Times* promptly panned it as sophomoric and dull. In a more forgiving world, an ancient bad review like this would disappear into the archives. But given Burns's failure to write another book, or article, or blog, or even letter to the editor, this review is the only thing that comes up when you search for him.

"So," Burns says, his tongue finding an inflamed part of his lip. I imagine he must be jealous of McDougal—and, quite possibly, jealous of all the candidates who've come through this door today, hope in their eyes, recent publications cluttering their vitas. He gives it away, wears the tight-skinned look of the frustrated and overlooked.

"I loved your book," I say, my last-ditch effort to save this interview.

I really need this job. I'm not making enough money copyediting. What else am I qualified to do after ten years writing and publishing stories? Essentially, I have a pedigree in the field of wonder. Useless, useless, but I can't afford another degree, I can't not work, and I can't leave Portland, not with my brother Arthur's situation. *The Boy with Wax Wings* is indeed a sophomoric and dull read. It features a young, aspiring writer who yearns to please his father, but instead, thinks a lot.

Burns sits back and raises the wadded Dixie cup like a crystal ball. The shrapnel in his eyes doesn't melt. I have to hand it to him: his bullshit meter works well. He continues to look at me as if I've single-handedly sullied his reputation.

I begin to ramble on about my work. I've recently written a few essays about a forgotten female novelist. And I won a small literary prize for a short story last year. Of course, I also have the novel I'm working on, and my two published story collections. Of course, too, there's all the teaching I've done, and the awards I won for that.

Before I'm done with my list of accomplishments, inflated slightly to impress, but spoken with a soft, small voice to woo, Burns claps his hands. "That was a fast thirty minutes, wasn't it? But it looks like we're out of time." McDougal has the paper clip out again. He's bent it into a long stick and has started scraping his teeth with it.

John Dutton looks at his watch. "Oh, well, yes, I suppose we should be moving right along, but Imani, it has been a pleasure meeting with you. The committee would like to thank you for flying all the way out to Denver for this interview. Oh, wait, let me just fetch you a packet we're giving to all the candidates. It's just a little information about the university." John Dutton goes over to a battered duffle bag near the nightstand and rummages around. The phone on the desk begins to chirp—a bizarre sound, more like a waning fire alarm than a ring.

Burns looks at it, and then accusingly, at me. McDougal has a second paper clip now, entwined with the first.

Burns heaves a sigh and gets up to answer it. "Yes," he says into the black receiver. "Oh, hello Audrey." He grabs the phone base, as if he could whisk it out of danger. "Excuse me?" He stands facing the bureau. In the mirror, the shadows beneath his eyes are darker. He looks forlorn.

Dutton hands me a stack of shiny brochures and a map of the city of Portland.

"I actually live in Portland already," I say. John Dutton blinks. "Never mind," I say. "Thank you." John Dutton holds his arm up toward the door.

I don't think I'm landing this job. Already, Arthur and I share his small studio apartment. We never eat out. He has a rare, terminal blood disorder. Before he got so sick, he groomed dogs. He never had insurance. The treatment he requires costs us far more than our rent, and we only have two thousand dollars left of our mother's death benefits. I make enough to pay rent and the minimum on the credit card. But we need a real salary. I need a real job.

"There's a gunman in the hotel." Burns says. He reaches up to his ponytail and yanks the rubber band out. His hands shake a little, whether from the news or the Red Bull, it's impossible to know.

"Excuse me?" says Dutton.

"No way," says McDougal, a grin spreading across his face. McDougal has opened a small carton of chocolate milk, which he drinks with a straw.

"That was an emergency alert from the hotel. It said there's no reason to panic, the police are on their way and the man will be apprehended, but everyone should stay in their rooms with their doors locked."

"Nice!" says McDougal. He laughs silently, a little pink hole opening in the thick hair of his beard.

John Dutton walks over to the door and locks it, then slips the top deadbolt into place. Outside, a sea of people streams from the rotating hotel doors into the sunlight.

McDougal leans down and unties his Doc Martens. He wears threadbare argyle socks. "So, Imani, take a load off. Anyone want to watch some TV?"

"What kind of idiot would try to rob a hotel?" asks Burns. His hair frames his face like a girl's. "Nobody's walking around here with cash. A hotel is a stupid place to bring a gun. Plus, it would be too easy to get trapped on one of the floors once the police came."

"Maybe it's not a robbery," says McDougal, the edges of his beard signifying a grin. "Maybe it's more of a sniper situation."

John Dutton shakes his head.

McDougal turns and gazes at the window. He pushes the filmy under-curtains away, then he lets out a giant belch.

Though maybe I should feel panicky, I feel a little optimistic. No other candidates will get this experience, this bonding time with these men. Six hundred and seventy-four applicants. With those odds, there's more than an element of dumb luck in getting the job. This, a gunman loose in a hotel during the thirty minutes I had to state my case, is the definition of dumb luck.

"Well, I guess we have more time to chat," says John Dutton. "Why don't you go ahead and take a more comfortable chair, Imani." Dutton stands and relinquishes his plush armchair.

"You have lipstick on your teeth," McDougal says.

"Raphael!" says John Dutton.

"She does!"

I quickly rub it off with my thumb.

"You had it on the whole time," says McDougal, grinning. "Like you were gnawing on crayons."

"Oh, well that's embarrassing."

"So, Imani," says Dutton. "What sorts of things do you read for pleasure?"

"Did you hear that?" McDougal says, turning his ear toward the door. We all listen, but only hear the hum of the minibar fridge.

"Oh, for Christ's sake, John," says Burns. It's definitely the Red Bull now. His eyes bulge, and he looks like he might go shooting through the ceiling. The can has fallen over onto the stool and nothing leaks out. He turns his intensity my way. "You're not stupid. You know this interview is a formality. Why don't we just stop the charade."

John Dutton's face opens and stretches. I can see him imagining the font I will use when I email the complaint letter to the Dean.

McDougal shrugs and grabs a paper bag hidden by the nightstand, pulling out a large bag of chips. "Hey, Imani," McDougal says, breaking my name into its clear three syllables so his lips and tongue get a little workout. "Don't take it personally. We actually thought you were black because of your name. The next girl coming in is Indian, and then we've got a Latvian dude and a Chinese girl."

"She a Filipina woman," says Dutton, his voice tiny.

The chips McDougal chews sound like they are made of tiny microphones.

"Whatever. Filipina." McDougal loses his train of thought here, sucking hard on his straw and marveling at his paper clips.

"My mother was in the Peace Corps in Kenya," I say dumbly. "That's how I got my name."

"Right on," says McDougal. Then he does that thing with my name again: Ee-mahn-ee.

"We have to consider diversity," says John Dutton, weakly. "We have a mandate."

"Eeeee-maw-neee," says McDougal. "Do you want a little tip, Eeeeemawn-nnnee? Don't be so desperate. You look desperate with that folder and that suit."

Burns glares at McDougal, indignant at having been outshone yet again.

"Shut up, McDougal," says John Dutton.

The Red Bull has started to make me feel nauseated and speedy, as though all my blood has expanded and now races around my body, pursued.

I grab my coat, but I can't leave. And so, I set it down.

"I'm just helping her out. I think I'm going to go take a bath," says Mc-Dougal. "I mean, we could be in here for hours."

"I actually need to use the restroom," I say. I don't, but I see no other way to gather myself.

The Hilton bathroom gleams clean and white, but smells distinctly of asparagus pee. I reach over and flush McDougal's waste into the large Colorado sewer system.

Finally, a mirror. My hair looks fine—dark ringlets. My glasses have no smudges. No more lipstick stains my teeth. But this quest for cash and security has left something I can't wash off. It's made the sanguine into saccharine. I smile, but I don't mean it, and the flat, vinyl records of my eyes give me away.

And then it happens. A gunshot so close, it makes my heart fly up and hit the ceiling and then land, thwack, down in my gut. The room beats as my heart stills.

There is a gunman in the hotel.

Burns and Dutton both stand by the dresser, wide-eyed. McDougal throws himself to the floor and wedges himself halfway under the bed.

"Shh," says Dutton.

"Was that a gunshot?" I whisper.

"Was that a gunshot?" Burns whispers with a girly accent. "Of course it's a gunshot." We stand there quietly, listening for other sounds.

"Get out of there," Burns says to McDougal, who grunts and strains on the floor.

"I can't!" he says.

"You stoned idiot. Back out," Burns says.

"I can't move backward, you have to lift the bed!" McDougal says. Sirens whoop and wail their way toward the hotel. Everyone gets quiet again.

John Dutton puts his thumbs to his closed eyes and sits back down on his chair. Then he moves his hands into a slight prayer position, though it doesn't appear that he's praying. It appears, actually, that he has escaped altogether. A monk, a recluse, a man with a completely still mind. There might be something to Dutton—a kind of innate genius. If I were allowed to do anything right now, and perhaps I am—who is to say I'm not?—I would crawl inside of John Dutton and take up residence. I would live with his tidy closet, his roasts, his mashed potatoes and chocolate pudding.

"Don't laugh, you asshole," cries McDougal. "You have to help!"

Burns smiles conspiratorially at me, a slyness in his gaze. Then he remembers he doesn't like me and averts his eyes.

"Why is he under the bed?" I ask.

"That is the best question anyone has asked all day," says meditating Dutton.

"I need you guys to lift the bed," says McDougal.

"No one's going to be able to lift the bed, you idiot," says Burns.

"If you don't lift the bed I am going to die under here!"

"You aren't going to die," I say.

Burns looks at me without derision.

"What do you know about it?" McDougal cries.

"Well, since you asked. My brother is dying. That's why I really need this job. We have so many expenses. I know you didn't ask, but it's not just academic for me."

"What's wrong with him?" asks McDougal from under the bed.

"A rare blood disease."

"I'm so sorry to hear that," says Dutton. And he really appears to be sorry. Then, something happens that I don't see, and McDougal's foot flies out from the side of the bed and catches Burns in the ankle. "Ouch," says Burns and delivers a swift kick to McDougal's ass, wedged only partially under the bed.

"Ow!" screams McDougal. "Man, help me out. You gotta lift up the bed.

I got stuck under this bar down here. Don't pull my legs!" Burns leans down and tugs McDougal's legs. "No! It's my skull that's wedged under the bar! You'll break my head!"

John Dutton looks at me with sadness, with tenderness, and I think maybe he might say something soothing or wise, but instead he gets up and goes to look out the peephole. "There's a police officer in the hall," he says. "I think I'll ask for an update." He unlocks the door and sticks his head out. The police officer rushes up to the door, pushing Dutton aside, practically climbing over him.

Our policeman is sweating a lot. He wears white Nikes with an aqua sole and his shirt has a tear where the name badge ought to be.

"Shit, lock the door," he says, holding out a small silver gun somewhat awkwardly. Dutton backs up into Burns, who catches him and holds onto his arms. The kid goes over and locks the door, scanning the room, his eyes darting. "Don't do anything," the kid says.

Burns, John Dutton, and I back up toward the big glass window that seems, suddenly, to be exploding in the Denver sunlight. People still mill around down there. My heart beats in my fingertips.

Burns breathes nervously, the short staccato sounds, too close to my ear, the smell hammy. McDougal has crammed his legs under the bed somehow. He's disappeared.

Our gunman appears young. Twenty, if that. He looks completely terrified, which calms me down a little, though maybe it shouldn't. His sea-green eyes spark under flyaway eyebrows. He wears a fraying friendship bracelet on the wrist of the hand holding the gun.

"What do you want?" I ask. The kid looks at me, then at the closed door.

"Don't talk!" the kid says. "Why are there so many people at this hotel? I tried to get out. I was just here to scare my stepdad. This is his fucking gun. Goddammit."

"Please put the gun down!" says Dutton, now waxy white and trembling.

Burns stares at Dutton. "I'm not ready to die," says Dutton, a film of tears fogging his eyes. "I'm only just beginning to live!"

"Shut the hell up, Dutton," says Burns.

"I'm only beginning to live!" wails Dutton. The gunman looks even more afraid, pushing the gun from one hand to the other.

"Get him to stop yelling!" the gunman says.

"Seriously, Dutton, get a grip," says Burns.

"If you let me go, I promise to tell my wife about Gracie. I will stop. I will be a better man."

"Jesus Christ," says Burns.

"What is this place, who are you guys? Why are there so many people at this hotel?" the kid asks again.

"It's a conference for creative writers," says Burns. "Like poets and fiction writers. Authors who teach."

"Is that what you are?" asks the kid. He looks momentarily interested.

"Yes," says Burns. "Well, actually, the crying guy is a scholar."

The kid tilts his head and looks at us. "I always thought I could be a mystery author," he says.

"Do you write?" I ask. Burns glances over at me, surprised, I think, that I'm still there.

"No," says the kid. "I'm not good at it."

"Well, surely that hasn't ever stopped anyone," says Burns.

"Get in the corner!" the kid yells. "Jesus Christ, stop moving around!" It's true, Dutton has inched toward the dresser, a look of agony on his face. He quickly moves back toward us. The kid scratches the back of his own neck so hard, I think he might draw blood.

"They're after me," says the kid.

"I imagine that they are," says Burns. "What are you doing, exactly, with that gun?" The kid swallows hard.

"My stepdad is an asshole," the kid says.

We all three look at the kid as though he might say more.

"Is there another way out of this room?" asks the kid.

"Not literally, no," says Burns. The kid puts the gun in his left hand and wipes the right hand off on his trousers.

"Shit," says the kid. "Shit shit."

There is absolutely no movement from under the bed.

"What are you all doing in this room, anyway?" asks the kid. Why are there two of you guys and just the one girl? Are you having a threesome?"

"This is a job interview."

"In a hotel room?" The kid touches his fuzzy, aspirational goatee with his finger. "But wait, if you're writers, then isn't writing books your job?"

McDougal grunts from under the bed. "Right," he says.

The kid remembers the gun and points it at the mattress.

"What was that?" asks the kid. "Is there a cop under the bed?" His whole face contorts and his hand tightens on the gun. My stomach tightens along with it.

"No," says Burns. "Of that I am sure."

"I'm going to shoot that mattress!" says the kid, his voice trembling. "Unless you get out right now! I'm going to shoot!"

"Help me out, bro," says McDougal. One of his legs unfurls from beneath the bed. "These assholes won't help. I'm trying to get out of here. Can you lift the bed?"

"Why is there a guy under the bed?" The kid's chin weakens.

"That is a professor," says Burns, his eyebrows raised. "That is a professor who crawled under the bed because he was afraid and got his head stuck."

The gun's small eye moves from the mattress, to the space beneath it.

"In so many ways, it is impossible to believe, isn't it?" Burns asks.

"Everybody stop talking," says the kid. "I gotta think." He points the gun at Dutton, who weeps openly.

"If you don't help me out," he says, turning the gun on me, "I'm going to—" The kid shuts his mouth hard and scratches the back of his neck again. "I'm going to shoot whoever is under that bed!"

"Go for it," Burns says.

The kid goes to the window. He can't get out that way. He tries a locked door to an adjoining room. None of us have a key to it.

"You guys gotta help me out," the kid keeps saying.

I can hear people coming down the hall, but the kid, distracted by escape fantasies, doesn't hear them. If we can just keep him from doing something stupid for the next few minutes—

"Why would you want to write mysteries?" I ask him.

The kid looks at me for a second, before investigating a heating duct the size of a novel.

"It's a limiting form, don't you think? Most of them end the same way. There's a crime, then people solve it. That's the point. Right? But if you don't have that gun go off, then your story could be about anything."

The kid looks like he might be trying to suck a little marrow out of a stubborn bone.

The door comes crashing down. "POLICE!" we hear.

"Shit," the kid says. He crams the gun in his pants and drops to the ground, squashing himself under the bed from the other side.

"Where is he?" the officer in front snaps. He's an unevenly proportioned man—large on the top and skinny in the hips.

"Under the bed," says Dutton.

"Get out from under the bed!" the policeman yells. Our young gunman doesn't move. "Relinquish your weapon now!"

"Officer," says Burns. Then he notes the three other officers standing behind this one so changes it to the plural. "Officers, you should know, there are two men under that bed. One is a tenured professor."

The policeman looks at us like we might all begin to drool. Then he shakes his head, his lids low, like he's seen even this before.

"I'm stuck," says McDougal. "Officer, can you please lift the bed?"

"Both of you, get out from under the bed!" says the policeman.

The kid tosses his gun and crawls out after it. He's quickly cuffed. Three officers lift the bed up and free McDougal, who has chocolate milk all over his white shirt. We're told we must wait for more police to arrive so we can answer a few questions, the first legitimate interview of the day.

"My God," says John Dutton, lying down on the bed. "That was such a close call."

"That was epic, man, fucking epic. Did you see that?" McDougal's glassy eyes have a gleam, like a spotlight shining into a pile of broken glass. He can't seem to shut his mouth. "We were, like, under the bed together like in a fucking war movie, man. That was epic. That was incredible. Man, we are all so shielded from what is important. Did you feel that? Like you just all of a sudden knew things? I gotta find a pen," McDougal says. He begins racing around, turning over pillows and unwrapping hotel glasses, shaking the ice container.

"Is your brother really sick?" asks Burns.

"Yes," I say.

He nods, and puts a hand on my arm, squeezes it gently. "I'm very sorry," he says. His hand is heavy and warm. McDougal finds a pen, lunges for the wrappers from the glasses, and begins to write.

"You were fast on your feet there, Imani. *Your story could be about anything.* Impressive."

"Thank you," I say. Now that the gunman has gone, I feel myself shaking. Or maybe it's just my proximity to McDougal, now giving off the energy of an air raid siren, the pen's scratching like the talons of a frantic bird.

The Red Bull and adrenaline have mingled and begun to sing.

"Do you really want this job?" Burns asks. "You have to spend your life with these clowns. It's not very good pay. And the course load will break your spirit. You'll probably never write again. But, if you really do want to be part of the gang . . ."

There's nothing I can do to stop Arthur from dying. The story's in its last act, gun fired, bullet lodged. But all stories don't have to end this way. You can lose a gun. Sell it. Melt it as scrap. You can find a different way to go. It's just harder to do.

McDougal has filled one wrapper and started on the next. His chocolate milk stain has the unlikely shape of two wings.

I shake my head no.

BEAUTIFUL BURN

W e're all veering toward it anyhow, death and its choir and chorus, its circus of light. It's not as if there's a fork in the road. You might see a child holding chocolates in a goblet made of nectarines. You might see tongues of flame. You might see nothing at all. We'll each know at some point which fantasy holds true.

It's an unspoken thing that Aura—her eyes as big as sink plugs, her ears sticking out from the tinsel of her hair—will know sooner than she should, unless someone finds a way to halt her.

When I arrive at the bistro—I'm a little late—they're already seated. I see them from the doorway, my father upright, though shorter than the other two. Mindy and Aura each wilt away from him like petals revealing their stamen. "Traffic!" I say, setting the birthday card down by my father's plate. In my bag, I have a small present, but I'd rather wait until we're alone, if we're alone. He stands halfway and I lean down to kiss his cheek. "Hi, Jess," he says. He takes my head in his palms and holds it. His wife, Mindy, crinkles her eyes at me. Then her red lips open as the rest of her face puckers, Mindy's weird interpretation of sweet. "Jessica!" she says. "We thought you'd never arrive!" A thicket of shiny black beads decorates the flat, tanned acre of skin before her blouse begins. She pats my arm.

"Hey," Aura says. She takes her heavy blue bag off the vacant chair. It's a student's bag, crammed with notebooks, her laptop, something in a wadded brown sack. Aura always looks so hopeful when she sees me. Our fluttery hug has me holding, for just a second, her shoulder blades protruding like saddle horns from her back.

I can tell my tardiness didn't interrupt anything. I've intruded only on their particular brand of silence. "I really like the lamb here," my father finally says. "They do a nice job with it."

Mindy touches my menu. "Take a look," she says. "We're ready to order."

Our waitress has a nose ring with an unfortunate green bead hanging just below the edge of her nostril. She dutifully tells us the specials. Mindy orders fish. My father orders the slow-cooked rack of lamb. I order the mushroom risotto. Then, it's the moment of suspense, the little drama that everyone politely rides over. We look at Aura. She takes a finger and twirls her hair.

"I stuffed myself at lunch," Aura says. "So, I'll just get the asparagus."

Mindy's dimples appear in her forehead and under each eye, in her cheeks and chin. "Are you sure you don't want anything?" Mindy asks. Aura hunches forward. A tiny diamond looks trapped inside the hollow of her clavicle.

"I *am* having something," she says. "I'm having the asparagus."

The waitress takes the menu and turns.

"So, what have you been up to, Jessica?" Mindy asks. She picks up her water but doesn't drink.

"I got the full-time position I applied for," I say. I direct this toward my dad, but he appears to be studying the creases in his knuckles. It's been six years since my mother died, a long time, enough to mess with memory. But I don't remember my father being such a mute. He used to sit in my mother's studio while she cleaned brushes. Did he talk or just listen? I remember walking in on that scene, day after day, year after year. In pajamas, in shorts, or later in dresses that my mom would adjust, tugging down hems so I showed less skin. She wore her hair in two long ponytails, each ending with a curl. She never minded if you played with them, if you made one have the voice of a wolf and one the voice of a girl, if you made one chase the other and eat it. She would go on reading or drawing or cleaning a drawer. When she died, I was already living in California, and I guess my father looked around his life—his solitary if lucrative job, his house decorated from top to bottom with his dead wife's oversized lithographs of warped fruit and dark, knotted trees—and because of the silence, he heard that choir coming from a distance. He felt fear, deeper and subtler than he'd ever felt it. It shook every organ in his body. It made his fingernails go dry. And when Mindy smiled at him in the synagogue, when she slid her phone number to him on a thick white card, he didn't have a complicated set of thoughts. He didn't analyze or wonder. He grabbed.

"The one at the junior college?" Mindy asks.

"It's a four-year college," I say.

She sets down her water. "I didn't realize they taught clay at four-year colleges," she says. "That's terrific!"

Mindy loves to talk about my job. When I came a few months ago, she had a couple over for dinner at the house. "Jessica teaches clay," she said— "*clay*," like she's flinging the word with her tongue. The couple made interested faces.

"Clay!" the woman said.

"Ceramics," I said. Then they went back to talking about their gardens.

"Congratulations," my father says.

"Aura," Mindy says. "That lipstick's a good color for you."

Aura doesn't take the bait. She looks coolly at Mindy and smacks her berry-stained lips.

I've always had a soft spot for Aura. When Mindy went through the house, tossing every remnant of my mother—her hairpins and cut-off shorts, her paints and books, vintage purses, even some of her paintings, it was Aura who went in the dead of night and dug the good stuff out of the bags. I don't know how she knew what I'd want, how she knew which bags and notebooks to keep. But she did. She saved it all for me beneath her bed.

It's hard to believe she came from Mindy's womb, this girl with no makeup save the lipstick. Aura has dark hair, such a contrast to Mindy's streaky blond curls. Her eyes are grave, an in-between color—yellowy-brown where Mindy's are blue—and they're shaped to look sad.

"So, what do you hope for your sixty-second year?" I ask my father.

"Health, wealth, and wisdom," he says. It's his stock phrase. Asking my father questions is like hitting the knee with a mallet to watch the leg kick.

"We're going to a spa in Tucson," Mindy says. "Didn't he tell you? We leave on Monday." The waitress sets down a steaming basket of bread. My father reaches for a piece. He tears it in half, takes a bite from the crust, then abandons the rest on his bread plate.

My mother died a bad death, slow and painful and grim. I like to imagine that because of this, my father's death will be different, the death he'd choose. He'll stop for a pee during one of his annual mountaineering adventures, unhook the harness, and stand for a moment—a man held by gravity to the side of a mountain. That feeling of being where no one should be—the glory, the rush. Then, he'll slip, land on his rear and slide down the ice on the butt of his nylon wilderness pants. It will be a little bit fun, like a toboggan ride with no toboggan, and he will have a gut-flapping surge of adrenaline as his hands try to grasp the ice beneath him. That's his last feeling: fire and wind in the gills. He'll plummet off the edge of a crevasse into the endless gash of aquamarine.

Mindy rambles for a while about the resort they'll be staying at. Indoor hot pools, cold plunges, a cactus garden, mountain hikes. Aura taps her knee under the table. Then she touches the very bottom of each piece of silverware with her index finger three times.

I know that Mindy tried to get Aura on antidepressants. They found her an expensive psychotherapist in Portland. But Aura flushed the pills and sat silently, week after week, in the shrink's chair and so Mindy decided to believe that this was a phase, that Aura would simply grow out of it.

The food arrives.

"Aura," Mindy says. Sometimes I forget this—that Mindy can sound mothering, concerned. Aura is busy removing a poached egg from on top of her asparagus. It quivers and threatens to split, but she has the focus of a surgeon and gets the egg onto her bread plate without breaking it.

"Do you want this?" she asks me, gesturing to it.

"Not really," I say. She shrugs.

"I hate eggs," she says.

"Aur," Mindy tries again.

"What," Aura says.

"Didn't you go on a date last night?"

"No," Aura says. Mindy sets her jaw and picks up her knife. She slices a small piece of her salmon.

"Please just try it," she says, setting the fish on Aura's plate.

"I ATE," she says, pushing the egg to the center of the table. Aura turns to me and rolls her eyes. "How's Gabe?" she asks. She smiles. She's pretty when she smiles. Or maybe she's just pretty, pretty all the time with that large forehead, those perfect little lips. It's hard to say, now that a pineapple yellow is creeping around her edges. She's pretty the way a cartoon nymph is pretty. Pretty with an edge of scary, pretty preparing to leave this realm.

"Gabe's good," I say. "He's lobbying for a dog." The last time I was here, I heard Mindy call him "Jess's Jewish carpenter," which I suppose he is. He's a cabinetmaker, to be specific.

"Dogs are easier than children," Mindy says brightly. Aura ignores her, slicing her asparagus into discs, then again into half circles.

After dinner, Aura and I both head for the solace of the restroom. We lock ourselves in separate stalls. At the sinks, Aura turns to me. It's a miracle of the human frame that such frail tendons and bones can hold up a skull.

"Do you want to go for a walk?" she asks. "Maybe talk?"

I haven't spent that much time with Aura. I drive the five hours north to visit a few times a year, but she's busy with her life at the university—doing whatever it is that she does—measuring her arms and legs, trying to shrink herself down to the smallest possible person. The way she's looking at me, I feel curiosity and dread in equal measure.

"Okay," I say. We say good-bye to Mindy and my father, assuring them we won't be that long, that we'll all come back to the house for a nightcap, and Aura leads the way up to the park, past old houses into tall trees beneath the butte. I feel I can hear Aura's bones creak like an old porch swing. I imagine her hair falling to the ground behind us, strand by strand. Maybe the birds will follow us, cartoon birds for this cartoon nymph, and they will make Aura a nest of hair in which to finally rest.

"Can we stop here for a sec?" She swings open the door of the mini-mart and asks for a pack of Camel Lights. There's a candy bar display by the register featuring my favorite kind, the ones with the soft truffle filling that seem European, though they probably aren't. Gabe buys them for me whenever I'm stressed or having headaches or when he just wants to get on my good side. "Do you want one?" I ask.

Of course, what Aura's doing is repellent, but I can see how it holds a sort of glory. It takes extraordinary resolve. You must work in stages until the denial feels native to brain and blood. In this way, you bring the world closer to you. The mother who, for years, seemed to see only herself suddenly realizes that you have a will all your own—that she doesn't and can never own you the way she seems to own the men she marries and the various rings and condos they buy for her. And at the same time as the body shuts down, the soul begins to sing. Before this, you've been an animal—ingesting, digesting, excreting—but now, you've risen above. It must feel like your heart is riding a swift bird. So high up, so far above the flesh's petty needs.

We walk down the residential street on the way to the paved river path. It's late summer and just growing dark at eight thirty. The pewter water reflects shimmering orbs of streetlight. By a pedestrian bridge, a few boys pass a joint between them. One of them tries a catcall, but his whistle comes out at the same time as a burp and his buddies laugh. We continue past the lights of the mall on the other side of the river, down to a tiny path that leads to a curved embankment, hidden from the path by shrubs. We're not the only ones who've found this little beach. A few faded beer cans sit nearby and broken cigarettes grow soggy in the edge of the river water.

Aura takes off her cardigan and sets it on a smooth stone, her white dress even whiter against the darkening sky. She lowers herself with awkward grace, takes out the cigarettes, and with a doll's fingers, pulls the cellophane tab. She holds the package to me but I refuse. She strikes a match and the flame illuminates her face, the shine in her eyes. She breathes in and the cherry lights orange. I take out my chocolate, fold the foil back, break off a square. Aura studies me chewing it.

I take a set of ceramic beads out of my purse.

"Oh, holy hell!" she says. When she smiles, she reveals more teeth than seems right. She takes one in between her fingers. "For me?" she asks. The last time I saw her I told her I'd make her a set like the ones of mine she'd admired. They're not her usual style, more hippie-chic than magazine-cool.

They're pit fire beads. The new business cards I ordered say Assistant Professor of Studio Art, but really, I light fires in holes in the earth in order to stain clay. My students spend weeks slaving over beautiful objects—slab vases, complicated sculpture—rolling the sides even, making slip to hold the sides together, smoothing the creases with bone tools. They sit for hours rubbing a smooth stone over the surface of each creation, pressing down whatever grit remains. When their piece is smooth and dry, I tell them to bring in household burnables, whatever might emit crazy fumes when we light a match. You never know what will leave the most beautiful trace behind when it burns. Then we string these objects on white twine and wrap the sculptures like sloppy mummies. We drive all this out to the mountains, dig a giant hole in the earth. Then we light our fires, cover the pit, and wait. I tell them, you don't have control over this part. You prepared the surface, and now you have to let nature decide how to finish it. Some of them find this the most natural thing in the world. Others squirm. One or two, every year, can't bring themselves to put their piece in the fires at all, choosing instead to paint them with the glass glazes in the studio, burn them at controlled temperatures into colors they already know.

This year, one of my students tied flavored pork rinds to her piece. She'd made a vase with smooth cutouts, the edges burnished so they looked like the lips of babies. The other students eyed her skeptically, tying down their bits of lace and waxy paper.

The next day, when we unpacked the pits, hers sat proudly on top, streaked in oranges, reds, and rust, like it captured a subterranean sunset. Along its edges, blue and gray circles rose into each other. It's what anyone hopes for in a burn. "Oh my gosh," she said, brushing the ash from the piece. We sleep out there, in the mountains by our pits, and so she had that mussed and earthy look they get, my students, no matter how nicely they keep themselves the rest of the year. She held her piece up to the sky.

The other students began hunting through the ash for their pieces. But she'd thrown caution to the wind with that pig skin. And hers, hers was the most beautiful burn.

"These are so pretty," Aura says, clicking a few together in her palm. They came out gray, mostly, but flecked with black and a bright violet, brought out by some copper carbonate I sprinkled on the fire. I rarely make beads. They often break or roll away, but Aura's stayed nicely on the metal tree in there, as if they wanted to belong to her. I tug out a piece of long grass and take a bead, string it on. In silence, we string the whole thing. Then I tie it, as best I can, around her neck. Some of the grass splinters, but the knot holds.

"My mother's having an affair," Aura says, breathing out a thick stream of smoke. She's looking at her own hand on the rock beside her. I look out at the water rushing under the pedestrian bridge. The currents are fringed with white. I feel a momentary pang for my father.

For a little while, we sit there, both of us cross-legged, the cool of the rock permeating our clothes.

"Is that what you wanted to tell me?" I ask her. She turns and looks at me with her shiny eyes, then turns her head back to the water.

"Maybe you didn't want to know," she says. I take a small rock and toss it out there, watch it sink. The news doesn't feel like news. It feels like she's dragged me down here to tell me that rivers are made from water, that we breathe oxygen, that she has an eating disorder.

Yes, Mindy is having an affair. Every time I call the house, I get my dad. He's watching news or the baseball game. He's figuring out how to marinate fish. Mindy's at the nail spa, the coast condo. Out with her girlfriends. Visiting her sister. I never say anything. It's not the kind of thing my father and I discuss. In our world, you get to have your broken parts and keep them to yourself. I did try to warn him once, before he dressed her in white lace and gave her a ring, but he went ahead with it. He got the prize.

"Is she going to leave my dad?" I ask.

Aura hunches over her legs and shrugs again. "You'd like that, huh?"

"Not necessarily," I say. Aura twists her mouth and curls over her knees, holding the cigarette out in front of her. She stretches her white dress over her knees.

"My mother's such a bitch," she says, looking coolly ahead, then she seems to flinch.

"How do you know she's having an affair?" I ask.

"She's stupid about it," Aura says. "It's like she wants everyone to know. It's that guy from the gallery—the framer, Quentin. She talks to him on the phone all day long. You'd have to be blind not to see it. And even then I think you would."

This, I'm sure, is completely and totally true. And I wonder whether my father thinks about it, or if it's something he's made his peace with. At least Mindy's there, unlike my mother. At least when she's at the house, her heart ticks, her eyes blink. She coughs and smiles and yells. She's a big stain on his life, but it's better than a hole.

I can't imagine how Mindy will die. She's healthy as a mushroom in a dung heap. Her interests—pampering her feet and hands, trying on blouses—don't seem the lethal sort. She drives with grace and calm. What if she never dies? I've actually worried about this. What if she just lives on and on, past my father? She'll gleefully steam away my mother's flowered wallpaper, sell off my grandparent's china. And when I think of the ancient Mindy, stuck in my life, showering herself with goodies purchased with my could-have-been inheritance, I can't help it, I begin to get superstitious. I wish on eyelashes, the one white goat, whole sand dollars, wishbones, and the moon: don't let my dad die first. Please, whatever is out there, God, spirits, luck and fate—please, take Mindy first.

Aura has put her cigarette down and is dismantling a leaf, ripping it down to its waxy spine.

I'm on a rock, too, but mine is jagged. No matter which way I shift, my back tightens. Finally, I stand. I go close to the water and take off my shoes. If I grip the edge with my toes, the water runs just over the tips. It's freezing, this water. I look back to see Aura reorganizing the cigarettes in the package.

"What are you doing?" She looks up at me, but not for long.

"Nothing," she says, putting the last two back in. "Sometimes they're in a weird order."

"They're all the same," I say.

"If I put them in opposite order, well. It's hard to explain."

"What happens? If you change the order, what happens?" She flushes, looks up at me with such a strange look, the look you might give someone right before they kiss you.

"I just think, it's like, protective," she says.

"Protective," I say. "Like magical cigarettes?" I grab a stone from the embankment. It's the shape of a deformed heart, a shot of white running roughly across it.

When I turn to Aura, her head is on her knees.

"You okay?" I ask. She doesn't move. "Aura?"

In the old Grimm's fairy tales my mother bought at a tag sale, two siblings, a boy and a girl, wander deep into the woods on the instructions of a stepmother, and no one ever finds them. They simply cover themselves with leaves and die there. I loved this version, the feeling it gave to me—a scary sense of wonder and gravity, the idea that death could be so gentle and harsh and pitiless. The children looked smooth and sweet and the squirrels danced around them as the leaves fell from the trees and buried them forever. I begged for my mother to read it to me. But after a few times, she tossed the book.

But Aura's fine. Inside of her chest, a heart, complicated and furious and beating. My phone begins to buzz. I grab it from my pocket. Aura finally looks up.

"Where are you guys? Where's Aura?" my dad says. He sounds too loud, distracted. I can hear noise behind him—not restaurant noise, something beeping.

"Aura?" I say. I look at her sitting there, shining eyes in dark sockets, but before I can say anything he tells me to get to the emergency room. How fast can we get back to the car? It's Mindy. "Come right now," he says.

"Something's wrong with your mom," I say to Aura. She stares at me.

"I know," Aura says. "I was just telling you that. A lot is wrong with her." She stabs the cigarette out on the rock.

"She's in the hospital." Aura's nose rises, her lip hitching up. Her shoulders bend toward each other—you can see everything, all the mechanics under her thin white dress. "What are you talking about?" she says. She stands up, slipping on the rock and the grass string gives, the beads flying into the river. For a moment she seems like she might dive in to save them.

"We have to go. I'll make you more," I say.

Quickly, wordlessly, down the river path. Dusk turns to night too fast. The bushes crackle with rodents, or cats, or teenage boys, or homeless men. I can feel Aura beside me, her hand flying up every few feet to tap on her forehead in a way I want to put an end to. I would give anything to be back in California.

"What's going on?" Aura asks. My father stands, waiting for us, by a blue vinyl sofa in the ER.

"Your mom's getting a CAT scan," he says. He looks completely pale. "She probably has a blood clot in her lung."

I've never seen my father cry, and he doesn't betray me now, but there's a look in his eyes I remember—a blank fear that lives in the dark area in his pupil; it comes screaming from that tiny hole, sending ice down the edges of my bones.

Aura's knees wobble. She opens her school bag and then she closes it. Something isn't right with her. She taps and taps and taps on her forehead. I can see a tremor working its way through her, out of her.

"Aura," I say, but she buckles at the knees, the bag swinging forward, pulling her. I grab and my father grabs but we both miss the mark, and she cracks her head on the metal coffee table.

"Jesus Christ!" my dad hollers. I have not seen him holler in years. He has Aura in his hands, some blood on her forehead now on my father's wrist, turning the cuff of his shirt vivid. I can feel myself moving toward the receptionist, but she's already moving toward us. A nurse lifts Aura, ushers my father back behind the swinging hospital doors. The lights shine from small circular fixtures. The ER has a low ceiling, a pale green floor with swirls of gray—a migration of gray dove skeletons against a nuclear sky. I feel momentarily mesmerized by them.

I text Gabe and explain that I will call, that he should wait up for me—*there has been an emergency with Mindy*, I write. I don't want to say anything about Aura.

The doctor explains that they're going to run some tests on Aura, too. Her heart, her kidney function. They want to monitor her—a good thing this happened, the doctor says. She's dangerously underweight. My father stands, fists balled, resolute. They tell us that both of them should be fine under the right care. We wait for a while. My father talks to Mindy while I read magazines. Aura tells both of us to fuck off, to leave her alone.

"Just go home and get some rest," the doctor says. "This could take several hours."

I watch the dark stands of fir trees as we make our way up to the house, the moonlight now falling in silver strands over the tops of them. Cars move past us, and we turn off the big road onto this familiar smaller one, driving down into a ravine where my father's house sits, wooden and mossy and angular. A long time ago, there used to be a swing set in the side yard, a canvas playhouse with big orange flowers painted on its side.

My father unbuttons his shirt as he walks to the master bedroom. I think of following, of offering to help, but what help can I be to him? And it bothers me, those memories of my own mother wobbling her way to that same bed. A vase that I made sits on the bookshelves. The decorative hole in its side looks, tonight, like the eye of a fish, bored with its primordial knowledge. I reach out to touch its smooth surface.

"What a day," my father says. He rubs at his eyes with the back of his hand. He looks at a pile of mail on the hall table, but he can't bring himself to pick it up. He rubs his eyes again. Then he makes his way to the kitchen. I can hear the rattling of the liquor bottles.

"I have something for you," I say, extracting the present. "Happy birthday."

He raises his brows and takes the tiny package. It's an old photograph, now carefully matted in an antique silver frame. My mother has her head half turned, her face slightly blurred, she's holding me at the top of a slide. My father stands next to her.

I have no idea who took this picture. It's not, technically, very good. We're smeary with movement. My mother holds me below the arms, but she will, in the next moments, let me go, sending me plummeting down the shining surface to a pile of wood chips below.

He holds the picture out, looks at it at arm's length, sets the small frame down on the counter. We stand silently, all the possible words drying up, wicked back into the heavens to rain on someone else.

THE HEALING ROOM

The high basement windows of the Healing Room send sheets of sunlight into the water. My students avoid the lit sections, tucking themselves into darker spots where the medicinal herbs have migrated like leaves in a windswept pool. Natalie flicks a bit of lavender off her chest. Ty ignores the small buds as they drift toward him and cling to the thick black hair of his arms. Terra studies, with fanatical focus, the pattern of the gold leaf on the mint-colored tiles. Ronald sits outside the water, his legs dangling in, his neck looking too thin to hold up his head.

Natalie, Ty, Terra, Ronald. These are not my only students, not my brightest students, not my favorite students, but Paulette, chair of our department and interim dean, mandated the trip. She came to these tubs a few months ago and returned ecstatic. Her thoughts, she claimed, became more creative as a result of the rituals. She was able to embrace complexity more thoroughly. We're a small college, known for emphasizing personal growth and creativity over "straight academics," which is another way of saying that we'll admit anyone who applies. Paulette felt the Healing Room would be perfect for some of our slow-to-flourish kids. So, she founded a scholarship, The DeCourvier Scholarship for Special Potential Students.

And it's their special potential we're locating today.

Natalie's goiter is why she's here, why she eats her dinner alone under a tree in the courtyard, mumbling to an imaginary friend. It sits there on her neck, a big flesh-colored leech.

"It's creepy quiet in here," she says. I can see Natalie's dark nipples through the white fabric of her swimsuit. "Maybe we should sing."

Natalie's face opens into earnestness when she speaks. Her eyes grow animated and her hands nip at the air. When she finishes, though, her body takes on a robotic stillness.

The students can't agree on a song, so Natalie sings quietly into a pretend microphone, twirling a lock of hair around her finger, while the rest of us sit. The words are imaginary, soft to the ear.

The lore surrounding our illustrious department head, Paulette De-Courvier, is that during the 1960s, she lived on a nudist colony in northern California. The other rumor is that at forty, she took a vow of celibacy, a self-inflicted sentence that she's served, religiously, for almost thirty years. Of course, I've never spoken with Paulette about this. She does our teaching evaluations and our scheduling. I try to stay on her good side.

"Youbetterstopthat," says Ronald. Ronald rapidly cycles through frightening highs and depressive lows. He's probably bipolar, but he refuses to go to Psych Services to be officially diagnosed. Graying skin darkens the area below his eyes and his mouth hangs slack, but by the end of the hour, he's likely to be as pert as a watered tulip, his eyes ablaze with God. He will tell me, while gripping my arm, that he has been chosen for things greater than I can imagine. He will say he will win 700,000 dollars from seven sources and will buy seven cars. He'll say we are born seven times to seven holy mothers. And I'll nod and feel a real and vital terror, which is always how it goes with Ronald. We're all lucky, I think, that he hasn't come with seven guns and blown us all to seventh heaven.

I have experience with the Ronalds of the world, but Paulette doesn't want to hear it. "You're not working in the prisons anymore," she says. "Now you are working in hope."

Hope is the god Paulette believes in. She has candles with the word glued to them in glitter, a batiked scarf announcing it in scarlet. If you want to buy Paulette a birthday gift or a holiday present, her proclivity makes it easy. The painted rock, the etched pendant—these can be found at the New Age shops on The Plaza. Hope itself, well. I guess that's what we're all doing here.

Ronald is in the dark cycle and his head won't lift.

"Youbetterstopthat," Ronald says again.

"She's just singing," says Ty. Ronald shakes his head in a slow no.

"I sang when I was a young child," says Terra. What a face she has. It reminds me of old plastic baby dolls, her features correct, but frozen. You can see her entire iris all the time. "I used to sing children's songs when I was young and living at 269 Heather Court. When we moved to 38 Madison Street, I sang Beatle's songs with my father. For instance, I sang 'Love Love Me Do.'"

According to her student file, Terra spent all of her life before college in a program that taught her skills to deal with the non-Asperger world. In class, she folds her hands in front of her on the desk after she speaks to signal the completion of a thought. She does this now, pretending to rest them on the surface of the water.

"Would you like to hear the lyrics?" she asks.

Ty squeezes his hands together and makes farty sounds with the air pockets. A geyser erupts from his clamped hand. The spray hits Natalie on the side of her face. Ty freezes.

"Love love me do," Terra begins. "You know I love you. I'll always be true—"

"Youallbetterstoppit," says Ronald, leaning forward, his lidded eyes turned toward the water, his shoulders hunched forward. Terra closes her mouth hard and two tiny dimples punctuate the corners of her lips.

"What's the matter, Ronald?" I say. Ronald jerks his body back against the tub and lifts his top lip, exposing his gums.

"You should learn to be less rude," Terra says, shaking her index finger at him.

Ronald doesn't move. He doesn't even breathe.

When I interviewed for this job, almost two years ago now, I met Paulette in a small hotel room at an academic conference in Denver. She sat alone, the department chair and committee all in one, a silk brocade shawl draped over her shoulders. She wore bright yellow plastic glasses and orange beaded earrings. Bits of lace edged her sleeves and the hem of her skirt.

"It is not a traditional job," she explained, her silver pen poised over her notepad. I nodded eagerly. Mine was not the traditional academic trajectory. This, Paulette explained, separated me: wheat from chaff. I expected her to ask how I'd found my way from a graduate degree in English to a career in corrections, but she didn't ask questions, only stared first at me, then at my curriculum vitae. Then she stared at the floral curtains and the white pillows. I watched her lightly creased face, the corners of her eyes scrunching and unscrunching, trying to decipher the various expressions. I'd applied to twenty-two teaching jobs at colleges and universities, and this was the only interview I'd received.

"You need a change," Paulette finally said, setting the tablet down on the small chaise lounge. Her ruddy cheeks looked like storm-dampened desert clay. Her blue eyes had a measured and reptilian coolness.

"So, then we'll try it," she concluded in her trumpety way. I felt like she knew me. It's embarrassing to say it, but she seemed to see me in a way that nobody had seen me, not for so many years. I imagined she knew the feeling I got each morning when I got into that uniform and performed those elaborate security rituals and unlocked the heavy metal doors. She knew the power of looking into a person at a vulnerable moment. She was, after all, looking at me this way.

Of course, this wasn't the job I'd imagined. You would have to be on drugs to imagine this job. But this is the job I got.

All this time, Natalie's soft song has progressed. She hoists herself up onto the edge of the tub and concludes with an upbeat, jazzy coda. Her thin arms rise to twist damp ropes of hair into a bun. She fastens it expertly with other hair. The goiter shimmers and I have to look away.

"Pretty earrings," Ty says.

"Thanks," Natalie says. "They're not real. Just glass." She traces the outline of the stone with her pinky.

"They look real," says Ty, his mouth in a wet small smile.

Ty doesn't belong with these kids. His ailment seems only to be the thick dark hair crawling like Spanish moss across his near-albino skin. If it weren't for the way he shines in the light, like a stallion or a bed of kelp, he'd just be that kid—that kid that played D&D and stayed up late writing sappy but observant emails to a female version of himself.

"Does anyone want to play a word game?" he asks. "If I say a word, you can then say a word that relates, starting with the last letter of the word I say. Like, if I say banana, it ends with "A" so—"

"APPLE!" shouts Terra. Everyone shifts slightly. Terra beams—those doll eyes shedding so much enthusiasm, no one knows quite what to do.

Ronald shakes his head. "You're all crazy," he says. He slides into the tub and leans back, setting his head against the tiles. His breathing is slow and rhythmic. With his eyes and mouth shut, he really could be normal. In fact, he might even be handsome.

My students startle when a bell dings over a set of intercoms in the Healing Room. Inexplicably, Ty claps his hands. The laminate instruction manual, or The Soak Map, as it's called, explains that now we are to put on our kimonos and sandals, and congregate in the fenced yard for a brief meditation prior to the tea ceremony. We do as The Map instructs. Terra ties her kimono belt into a giant, sagging bow.

We gather around the chiminea, allowing the smoke into our faces. The objective of this meditation, explains The Map: visualize your essential self.

"It's freezing," Ronald says. It is cold. It's spring, but winter remains in the breeze. Flagstone and gravel cover the yard. A green umbrella shades a small wrought iron table.

"Here," I say, "stand here." I point to the place right in front of the fire. Ronald shakes his head.

"I don't understand what we're doing," says Natalie. "What's an essential self?"

"It's your soul," says Terra, very matter of fact. "Like the dream machine inside your brain." Natalie pulls her face into a pucker.

"Huh?" she says.

"I have a jacket inside," Ty says to Ronald. "I'll get it for you." And without waiting for a response, he wanders back into the building.

"I have a jacket, too," says Ronald. But he makes no move toward the door.

Bo, the manager of the Healing Room, has materialized from behind a small shed. His bald head shines in the sun. He lacks eyebrows and lashes. It's probably alopecia. What a contrast to Ty, he is. Maybe the world balances itself this way—one man robbed of hair and the other bestowed with so much, it becomes a liability.

Even in the cold, Bo wears a T-shirt with the sleeves ripped out to showcase his bulging shoulders and biceps. A tattoo of an eagle sits exactly where it should on his shoulder.

"How y'all doing?" he asks.

"Fine, thank you," says Terra, teary from the chiminea smoke. "How are you?" The wet tips of her hair make small dark s's down the back of her kimono.

"Need anything?" He's holding a ceramic pot of tea. Terra grimaces. The correct response to "How are you?" is not another question. Poor Terra. The world is a knot. She'll spend her life trying to loosen it.

Terra doesn't like me. She's filed three formal complaints to Paulette, which is why Paulette put her under my watch. We need to heal this, too— our little puddle of friction. The source of her discontent remains murky, but every time she turns in an essay, I can barely swing from one obtuse sentence to the next. So, I hand it back with the customary note that she needs to start over with help from library tutors. But Terra doesn't believe she needs tutoring. Terra believes that the soul transfers its heat through the pen and that I am building a fence around it, her soul. Her dream machine of the brain.

"Everyone's a critic!" she'll hiss when she receives the note. Then she marches to Paulette's office and details for her the entire lesson plan I taught that day, signing off that she is "most dissatisfied!"

"Are you guys ready for tea?" I ask. Ty holds his coat, an outdated ski jacket with lavender shoulders. "Here you go!" he says, handing it to Ronald.

"I'm not putting that thing on," Ronald says. And I see it happen, the wind inside him kicking up, the lidded eyes opening and that weird glow coming on. His hands twitch. He licks his lips.

"Follow me, people," Bo booms. The students line up and follow him up whitewashed stairs.

An avalanche of light spills over white and rose-colored pillows. In the center, a small table rises like a marble mushroom, set with Japanese teacups.

"Get out of my spot," Ronald says to Ty. Ty grins and moves to the next pillow. I imagine Paulette on these floor pillows, moisture caught in the crevasses of her skin, breathing in the scent of wood, lavender, mixed with must. My image of Paulette slowly morphs. My mother looked nothing like her. She was black-haired, bird-boned, with teeth the size of headlights. What would my mother have said about these rituals, these activities that are supposed to unlock the doors to living? There are no doors, she would probably say. It's what she used to say whenever I paused as a kid, before I jumped into a cold pool or went to a junior high dance. There's no door. You're making one up. Just go.

At first, I loved my job in corrections. I didn't love my colleagues. In general, correctional officers are not an inspired bunch. But I liked the Warden, a former literacy instructor herself, and I liked the steady pay, and the promise of a pension. After the high-minded hush and polish of the wood-paneled seminar rooms, I liked the no-frills officer break room with its piles of generic soda and stacks of local newspapers. But the access to something real, that's what I valued most. While most of my peers were shut away in libraries, writing and rewriting obscure ideas, I was in the trenches, in the space between life and death, sanity and insanity, hope and despair. I saw the women come into the wings with their eyes blazing with fear or dull with dope. And I saw them days later, sometimes angry, but often porous, momentarily open to new things.

My favorite inmate, Nita "MamaLo," had been transferred to our facility due to gang activity down south. MamaLo, who wore the blue prison uniform as if it were Hermes, sang gospel on Sundays and led aerobics classes in the tiny library. MamaLo had perfect skin, the kind of skin they airbrush to mimic, the kind of skin teenagers aspire to but never get. It looked like hide stretched over a drum, but the color was a beautiful, sun-soaked brown. She had magnet eyes that grabbed securely onto objects, faces, other eyes. Her muscles didn't twitch, her hands never fluttered. The women followed her around the facility like ducklings.

True, MamaLo had killed three rival gang members with her bare hands. But, MamaLo could talk politics. She was always changing the channels on the communal television from game shows to CNN. After I overheard her lecturing a group of women about the horrors of hormones in chicken, I brought her a couple of my readers from classes I'd taken as an undergraduate—urban studies, political movements, ecology—and she underlined the interesting passages, copying sections into a small black notebook she kept under her mattress.

We used to chat, frequently, outside the bathroom, or in the caged-in smoking area. She told me once that she never believed in God, and that she wasn't about to start believing in any of the gods they offered in here, but sometimes, when she was very quiet at night, she could feel her mother come down and visit her, brush her cheek with her finger. "That's as close a relationship to God as any of us are ever gonna get," she said. I'd lost my mother when I was seventeen. MamaLo had lost hers at sixteen. We exchanged these ages and nodded quietly, MamaLo ashing her cigarette into a leaf that had somehow made its way inside the cage.

"I like you," MamaLo said to me. She was leaning back in an old plastic chair, playing keep away with the television remote in the small communal area the female inmates shared. "You're a really different kind of person. But I gotta ask you something."

"Sure," I said to her.

"I gotta ask you why you're working here? You got this major degree. You got this big brain and a nice face. Nothing's wrong with you. We're all here because we have to be. But you're here because you want to be. That's pretty messed up. There's a whole big world out there and you're choosing to be in lock-up."

"It's complicated," I said.

"It isn't complicated," MamaLo said. "That's what's crazy about it."

"I feel useful," I said. She shook her head.

"Do you know how many people are gonna get out of here and change? Do you know how few even have that choice?"

"I feel comfortable here," I said. "I feel part of something."

MamaLo turned to look at me, a small shine of amusement in her dark eyes. She moved her body in a yes motion and then tossed a TV remote to her friend, Kim.

Around this little table we sit. Bo has left us to our quiet musings. And it is quiet except for Ronald tapping his teacup with a fingernail.

Once we're done with the quiet time, we read our Soak Map to learn the rules for a game called Essence. To play, we choose a person and then all imagine an object that would signify their essential self. When the bell dings and it's time to open my eyes, I see Terra pouring over the description of the game, trying to understand.

"Who wants to go first?" They stare at me.

Ronald makes a sudden gasp. His mouth is open in soundless laughter, and the hollows in his cheeks seem too deep. "I'm looking at you," he says to me. His maroon tongue darts over his lips. "And I see some old bones." He's rocking back and forth on his haunches.

"Excuse me?"

"Dry old meatless bones," he says, clutching his middle.

In class, Ronald's either sprawled out, half-asleep, his lids too thick, or he's incapable of stopping a string of epithets or an evangelical fit. "Dead meatless bones," he spits out between spasms. "That never get touched, never get touched, never get—"

"Enough Ronald. That's disrespectful." I glance at Natalie for backup. Often, in class, she offers up the odd but stabilizing comment. But I'm surprised to see her face gnarling into a sneer.

"Are we supposed to be *respectful?*" Natalie asks.

"What?" I say.

"Because I know you don't respect *us*. You think we're dumb. You have to do this Healing Essences crap because we're the idiot crew."

"I don't think that," I say, but I can feel the flush of my face.

"Sure you do," she says. "You call on certain people in your class, the people you think are smart, and you avoid us. I don't really care what you think, but you should just know that we know."

Ty smiles mildly at the wall. Natalie loosens her hair, dragging it across her neck so it covers the goiter.

"I think you're smart," I say.

I do think she's smart. Natalie rarely turns in her papers, but she makes curious connections between unrelated subjects. I don't call on her because I don't have to; she blurts.

Terra, on the other hand, well, she's a survivor. I respect her tenacity and her fierce desire to belong. But she struggles with the literary segments in class because she can't understand nuance. And no matter how many tricks she learns—niceties or gestures—nuance will not be among them. I'm sure she experiences things beyond the scope of my imagination, but if we are talking about traditional measures of intelligence, well, what can I say? And Ronald might be smart, but how can I know? How can I get beyond his odd obsession with seven? If I could stop him inside the moment of metamorphosis—that slim second when his eyes go from lidded to bright, I might see something unusually human. I might be able to hold, for a moment, his story.

But he sits there on his pillow, jerking his arm, smiling. His eyes bug out, just slightly, as if they are watching the best action scene in a movie. He has strong, even features. I can imagine his mother's delight when she sees him approaching from afar—the fantasy that he is her whole and perfect progeny.

Bo materializes from the stairwell. "Everything okay in here?" he asks. The skin rises where his eyebrows should be. He's concerned about this group. From the get-go we've looked a little haphazard, a little difficult to manage. Ty's swimsuit ripped and he needed a new one. Terra asked four times whether there was chlorine in the water and if so, exactly how much and from what company.

"Everything's fine," I say to Bo.

"Everything's fine," Natalie mimics. Bo doesn't seem to hear.

"Groovy," he says, waving his large hand at us. "You all just sit as long as you like and leave the cups there."

"Groooovy," says Natalie.

"What kind of tea is this?" Terra asks. Natalie pushes her cup to the middle of the low table. A small brown vase holds a marigold, its petals dry as corn flakes.

"Alright then," says Natalie, "maybe you can clarify something for us, Ms. Professor. What *is* the purpose of this scholarship?"

What is the purpose of this scholarship? What would Paulette say, ensconced in scarves and ponchos. Did she really experience epiphany of some sort, or was she simply taken by the feel of the silky water on her skin? What did she see when asked to visualize her essential self? A lone wolf? A black-berry hemmed in by thorns? A pearl buried deep inside the oyster?

And what am I doing here, wrapped in a blue kimono, mentoring the problematic children of people I've never met? One night when I was on duty at the prison, I opened the janitorial closet to see MamaLo on her knees in front of my superior officer, a man everyone called Pudge. MamaLo had just finished, and I watched her lips close, the movement of her jaw as she swallowed.

"Get out of here," Pudge said, zipping up his uniform, his hand clumsy on his billy club.

In the hall, my heart dangling too low in my chest, I listened to the click of something electric, the equally whitewashed silence of my own thoughts. Pudge walked quickly past me, but MamaLo paused. "Don't worry about it, Hon," she said. "Now you're part of something." She grinned at me, childish-ly, her eyes a little gleeful.

And that's when it really dawned on me. MamaLo had killed people with the power and strength of her own hands. She had actually done this. It wasn't a story, it was real. It made my own hands feel so warm and small and weak.

I went home that night with a dull ache in my head. I didn't know her. I didn't understand her, and how could I pretend to help, correct, and educate people whose lives I only marginally understood?

When I gave my notice, MamaLo found me on my way out. "Have fun out there," she said. "Send me a postcard. And some cash." She smiled and she winked.

Bo comes in with something green in a bowl. He sets it down in front of us. "I almost forgot!" he says. "This'll cleanse the intestine for proper digestion."

"My intestine is clean," Ty says, after Bo is out of earshot. "At least last time I checked."

"So why are we here?" Natalie asks. I can feel all eight of their eyes.

They know the answer. They know that the kids without goiters, the kids with apples in their cheeks, faded bandanas tied around glossy hair—these kids aren't given The Scholarship. This is the special room, the short bus.

"It's a gift from Paulette," I say. "It helped her get her potential unblocked."

"Words flow from God," bursts Ronald. "Block, lock, tickidy, tock. Right from the heart of the holy. Spirit. Hear it. Hear it spirit. Words are from emotion, emotion flow. Down low, here we go." He is shaking his hand in front of his face. His foot jerks.

"You shouldn't talk," Natalie says to him. "Like, ever. You just shouldn't talk." She gathers force, then reaches for the marigold and pulls it from the vase. She yanks off the flower's head and tosses it toward Ronald. He slouches over, puts his head in his hands.

"What do you think you're doing?" I ask.

"When I get back to my dormitory, I plan to take a shower and brush my hair a hundred times. A hundred times for healthy hair," Terra says. "Do you know what my surname means?"

This is an exercise I had them do, look into their surname.

"What does it mean?" Ty asks.

"It means beautiful conqueror."

"That's amazing," I say. "What's the origin?"

"Who cares?" Natalie says. "Nobody cares about Terra's origins." Her eyes are narrow and she leans forward.

"Natalie," says Ty. He puts his hand on her arm. His dark hair doesn't shine in here; it looks flat, like a dusting of feathers.

"Are you sure it doesn't mean big ugly retard?" she says.

"Natalie! That's inappropriate," I say.

"I am not retarded," says Terra. "I have Asperger's Syndrome. It is a condition, but I can do everything you can do." Her eyes fill with tears, but then all the water drains right back in. "I would like to go home now," she says. She looks around, presumably for her things. Then she tightens the belt of her kimono, and heads down the stairs.

"Why are you covered in that hair?" Natalie asks Ty.

"What?" he asks. She turns to face him, grasping the edge of the table with her fingers. Her nails are chewed to their pink quick.

"You need to cut it out," I say, placing the teacup back on the table. Natalie jerks her arm as if I've grabbed her.

"My mom says it's the fur of the angels," he says.

"Angels don't have fur," Natalie says.

"You don't know shit about angels," mutters Ronald.

"You need to calm down, Natalie," I say. "Or I'm going to have to report you to Paulette." She turns. And then she lifts her hair up and away from the goiter. She crawls up to me and puts her swollen, lumpy neck in my face. She smells familiar, like cottage cheese.

"This, this is why I'm here," she says. She takes the goiter and pinches it between her fingers. The skin is discolored there, like a ripening plum. My gut churns. "It doesn't matter what I know or what I do. All you see is this." I can feel Ty turning away from us, back to the wall. "This is all you see. You know what this is? A thyroid condition. A thyroid condition, that's all. It'll go away on its own. We're Christian Scientists and I have to let this go away. On. Its. Own."

"Okay," I say.

Natalie gives the goiter one last squeeze and backs up, back to her pillow.

Ty looks up at me and I feel a sloshing in my chest. He has large, weepy-looking cow eyes and they want me to feel happy, I can tell. His thin fingers flutter near his mouth.

"This isn't my idea of a good time, either," I say.

"Finally," Natalie says. "A little truth-telling."

Ronald has slid all the way to the ground, his long body curled over his hands, twisted into a strange looking prayer.

"I don't think there's anything miraculous in the water," I tell them.

"Me neither," says Ty.

"Of course not," says Natalie. "It's just regular water. I saw all the pipes. They're the same pipes that go to the sinks and toilets. They just add herbs."

I realize now that that's what she was looking at as she paced around the perimeter of the church earlier in the session.

"Besides, what do we all need to heal from? I mean, who are *you* to say who needs healing?" Natalie says. "Maybe *you* need healing."

One of my hands holds the other one under the table. I let it go, let the hand fall to my knee, feel its small weight. Ronald's intake of breath turns into a slight snore. A line of drool slithers down his chin.

"Except him, he needs meds," she says.

Terra returns from the bathroom, dressed in her outfit. She's fascinated by stories she heard in childhood—princesses and maidens. She wears a tiered skirt sewn up with sequins and a loose velvet top. Her barrettes have real dried roses sewn to their satin.

"I will wait downstairs by the door for you," she says. "Because I'm all ready to go." Natalie rolls her eyes.

"And you can't heal from something like that," she says as soon as Terra has vanished from view. "Everyone knows that. It's not a bruise, it's a brain."

"Hey," Ronald says. We're downstairs gathering our things. "Anyone seen my Raiders jacket?" This is perhaps the first totally average sentence I've heard him ask. But it's not the words as much as his eyes. There's a boy there. A boy looking for his coat. Terra points to a peg obscured by the open bathroom door.

"Behind there," she says. He walks over, puts the coat on. He sees himself in the mirror and puffs his chest out, lovingly pats his jaw.

"How're you feeling, Ronald?" I ask. He meets my gaze.

"I feel pretty good," he says.

Natalie has finished lacing up her boots and tying her white silk scarf around her neck. Ty looks at her. And not just looks—gazes. He wears a stupid smile and his hands are slack. Natalie senses Ty's gaze and she turns away with force, flipping her hair and bag to one side.

The road back to the college is desolate, peppered with sagebrush and dying cacti. Nothing impedes the view of the mountains. A hundred miles of desert looms before us. No one in the van speaks.

"OH MY GOD!" Ty yells. My heart leaps and my hands jerk from the steering wheel, sending the van over the double yellow lines. My reflexes kick in and I swerve back to the right side of the road, but too quickly, causing us to tilt at a frightening angle. I get it worked out, though.

"What?" I say, craning my neck, willing my heart to stop thumping.

"My intestines are clean!"

"Oh my God! Mine are too!" Natalie yells. And I can hear them giggling, Ty snorting ever so slightly. To my astonishment, even the humorless Terra is laughing.

"It's a miracle!" Natalie says. The three of them have their hands stretched toward the ceiling of the van. They are waving them in the air.

"Praise Jesus and tap water!" Natalie says.

"Praise Jesus and tap water!" Terra mimics.

"I'm healed!" cries Ty.

"If you spill that on my coat," Ronald says, pointing to Ty's apple juice bottle, "I'll beat your head in."

"Healed!" Terra shrieks.

"No, I'm serious," Natalie says in a husky voice. "You're healed." Terra goes quiet.

The setting sun lands in my vision, exploding in fiery light across the asphalt, temporarily blinding me. I press my foot into the brake—as if that will dim the sun—as if it's ever that easy to change things.

SOOTHSAYING

The clanking of the car's engine ceases a few miles out of town and Cliff and I settle into it, the wide quiet. We're told that here, high up and in fall, aspens turn whole mountains gold. I twist the knob on the radio, though it's been broken for years. We listen, instead, to rubber on asphalt.

For a while I watch the scrub, scouring the beige sand for coyotes or jackrabbits. Then, looking down I notice the specks of coffee and dust in the vinyl lining of the emergency brake. My husband, Cliff, stares at the road, the yellow lines finally disappearing. He's from the desert and so he likes this, this alien blue sky, the way the road out in the distance wiggles and turns into a lake. I'm from the coast. I miss the trees, the way they hide wires and façades, the way they block up the view.

Because it's quiet, because we are the only people we know here, Cliff and I argue. It's nothing serious. He leaves his clothes in the washer until they're dried to the sides and must be peeled away. If I ask him to take out the trash, he asks me to pick up my clothes. This morning we argued about eggs, whether when you poach one, you put vinegar in the water. Oh, the quiet— the big brown mesa out our window across which blows air and dust and birds, the way it is turning us toward each other, like opposing magnets. He's still sore at me for asking him if he ever poached an egg. "It's not what you *ask*," he said, leaning forward with his shoulders. "It's how you ask it."

Today, we'll find the aspens. But, Cliff seems to say with his jaw, with his arms locked in front of him like two table legs, this doesn't mean he forgives me.

"Let's play a game," I offer. Cliff pushes back into his seat, listening. I remove my feet from the glove box, leaving a dusty grid. "Tell me a story. Something I don't know about you."

He uses his thumb to flatten the hair above his sideburns. Last night I trimmed them, during a peaceful interlude, and now they look shorn while the top of his hair puffs up, a shiny mushroom. He's clearly wrestling with it—whether to succumb to the invitation, filling the car with friendly chatter, or to refuse, keeping the petulant, if ridiculous, chill.

Cliff watches the road for a while. He keeps mints in the cup holder and now he reaches for one. It crunches between his teeth.

We drive over a dead gopher and Cliff shakes his head slowly. He's a failed vegetarian, but the sight of roadkill makes him pensive.

"What kind of story?" he asks.

"I don't know. Something you've never told me."

"Give me a topic," he says. I touch his hand on the steering wheel, and briefly, he takes his other hand and puts it on top of mine.

"Injuries or scars," I say, because why not? He twists his lips.

"You already know about my scars," he says, which is true. He had a large mole removed from his thigh when he was young, and it left a raw pink line, which he sometimes claims is a shark bite. He has a small white storm of marks on his ankle from getting caught in some barbed wire.

"The next time we see a gas station, we have to stop," he says. "Did I ever tell you about Shane and the BB gun?" I watch the little black arrow on the gas gauge hover over the white square. The gas light flicks on.

"No," I say. "God, do you remember when everyone had a BB gun? A kid in my first-grade class had a BB embedded in his neck. You could feel it if you put your fingers on the right place." Cliff glances at the gas light. He takes another mint. When he chews, the hollows of his cheeks suck in, making deep caverns. He hasn't shaved. Little flecks of copper and gold wink from the indentation. "It was that kid, Todd, the one I told you about, the one whose mother brought in super-eight footage of his birth," I say. I'm thirty-four and still, whenever someone tells me they're pregnant, I conjure Todd's mom hanging from stirrups, screaming like her skin was on fire.

Cliff and I talk about having children, two maybe, even three, but it hasn't happened. Sometimes, at night, I pat at the space between us and say, here she is, our Josephina, our Noah, our little progeny. For a few years, Cliff played along, contributing geographical baby names: Topanga, Tonopah, Sierra. But now it's become routine, an airy joke. Often, he just ignores me.

He sees a sign and circles back to the last Allsup's before the mountains. Leaving the nozzle in the car, he walks into the mini-mart. The passenger seat won't move back, no matter how much I try to force it, and when I reach under to wiggle the crank, I find an empty wine bottle there, escaped from the recycling.

My mind flits to a story I heard in school, years ago. Apollo, god of light and music, is struck by the beauty of a sibyl. What will she trade him for one night in bed? She considers this. This is a sharp sibyl and she sees her chance. He's a god. What else to wish for but eternal life?

Time passes, though, and the sibyl has a change of heart. She doesn't want to sleep with him, doesn't want to hold up her end of the bargain. It doesn't take Apollo long to tilt the scales back in his favor. He's given her eternal life, but not yet eternal youth. So, the sibyl ages—and ages forever—growing smaller and smaller as she does. When she's finally as small as a grain of sand, she's swept into a bottle at the ocean's edge, trapped in a prison of glass.

It's moments like these, with a story in my head, that the absence of little Josephina is most pronounced. She appears, but in ghost form. I can almost feel her. Her fine hair is a version of my own, coppery with a corkscrew curl. She listens to the myth or the song on the radio and I feel a sweep of understanding. I will leave the world someday, but she will carry our history in these details. The time I told her the myth while waiting for Cliff to fill the tank. The way the sun warmed the plastic dash, the fungusy smell of the car. These things will crawl inside of her like seeds, becoming both important and frivolous, the way history does.

I would tell Josephina that a sibyl knows everything. She can see war coming to her country, she can see her friends in peril. If she were free, she'd have the power to change this, but she's not free. She'll see her predictions come true through the fog of sea-salted glass, growing even tinier, even more insignificant.

I want to die! she'll cry in her tiny voice. *I want to die!*

Cliff tosses a bag of chips at me.

"They only had that kind," he says. "Super Nacho Cheese with Jalapeño."

A cartoon animal on the front of the package looks like he'd like to lunge at my throat. I stick the chips by my feet. Cliff finishes up the gas.

I pick the bottle up and check it for sibyls.

"That's my emergency plan," he says, climbing back in. "Since I refuse to get a cell phone."

It takes me a minute to understand. "And float it in what ocean?" I ask. He shrugs.

"God will provide," he says. "Open the chips."

The bag's swollen from the elevation and makes a whooshing sound when I tug. The quiet happens again. Two cars pass, making wind. A large black bird hangs in the sky. We're headed up now, then down into a small canyon where some adobes are sprinkled at random, then up again, climbing the side of a mountain.

"It was in Reno," Cliff says. "When we lived in Reno, me, my mom, and that guy Ray."

I've heard about Ray. I imagine he was wound too tight, his jaw just skin over a series of pulleys and wires. Oiled black hair and an oiled black jacket and oiled black shoes. A belt buckle that sagged toward the floor.

"Well, Ray was married when he was seeing my mom. I told you that, right? He had this wife. I can't remember her name—Pricilla, Prissy—she came around every once in a while."

I put a woman with oily Ray. One of those women who lack moisture, whose faces stretch taught against bone. She wears a dress—no a waitress uniform. Light blue with an apron.

Cliff reaches for more chips. One has fallen onto his T-shirt, defying gravity. It sits there, cockeyed, at an improbable angle, like a small, invisible hand props it up.

"She got a boob job. That I remember." He shakes his head. "Is that even possible? Were people getting boob jobs in the late seventies?"

"I'd guess yes."

"Well, one day she came to the house to pick up her son, Shane. I guess Ray had joint custody or something. Shane stashed all these low-budget porno magazines in our shed, so we used to go out there." Cliff widens his eyes and makes a smooth, angel face. "Of course, I never looked at the magazines," he says.

"Right."

"Prissy was just some older lady, but that day she arrived with a rack like you've never seen. Made a big impression on me. I was ten." He takes another handful of chips. The rack doesn't fit with my light blue uniform. I try to reinvent her—polyester T-shirts? Low cut blouses? But now my images are muddled.

"Shane had this BB gun. These chips are gross. The jalapeño tastes like motor oil." Cliff tosses his handful back in the bag, then wipes his hand on his shorts, leaving a small orange dusting. "I have no idea if Ray got it for him, or if he borrowed it, or if it was from one of his mother's boyfriends. Because I remember a lot of boyfriends involved in this Ray thing. There was Ray, my mom's boyfriend, but then there were these huge guys with wolves for pets that tagged along with Shane's mother. And Ray would get really drunk and cry on the back porch and sometimes my mom would kick him out."

Cliff's hands clench and unclench around the wheel, his mind skimming over its own history.

"Shane had the gun," he says again. "And so, obviously, we had to go shoot some stuff."

"Obviously." I pick the chip off Cliff's shirt.

"Neither of us could drive yet. Shane put the BB gun in a duffle bag and we got on a bus out of town, this bus that went to the edge of a housing development. You could walk straight into nowhere after the last house ended."

"You were ten?"

"I know."

For a woman who soothed dying people for a living, who saw that life was temporary, Cliff's mother, Connie, was surprisingly oblivious to danger.

She dated men with gun racks, knife collections, and special radios. Once, she rode on the back of a motorcycle wearing nothing but a negligee. I met her two years before she died, after her exotic beauty had given way to a muted and puffed façade. She had the coloring of a Christmas dinner—ham and bread pudding, overboiled green beans. But photos of her young capture sharp shoulders and lithe arms, a butt poured into dark denim. In a few she winks, as if she knows a secret.

"Shane wanted to shoot lizards. So, we did. We shot maybe six of them. They were sunning on the rocks and we just picked them off. I don't think we missed even one." It's odd he doesn't cringe, this man who softens over the sight of a gopher smeared like jam over the asphalt.

"And then, the weird part," Cliff said. "Shane wanted me to take the gun. He put it in my hands and he dared me to shoot my own foot. I said no. He said it would feel good. I asked him if he'd done it, shot his own foot. And Shane pulled up his pant leg and showed me a whole mess of scars, a million tiny white bumps and lines." He reaches for the chips, but changes his mind. "Do you have any gum?" he asks. I don't. "Water?" he asks. I hand him my Nalgene. He drinks for what seems like a long time.

"And then?" I say. Cliff takes another swig of water and wedges the bottle between his thighs. He taps his thumbs on the wheel and curls his lips around his teeth. He sits there lipless, remembering.

"Shane got really intense. He took my hand and tried to force me to shoot myself. I didn't want to do it, but I was only ten and I wasn't as strong as him. Finally, he managed to get me pinned beneath him, but he couldn't hold me down and make me shoot at the same time. The gun was actually a little ways off in the dirt. Shane said he'd only let me go if I shot him. I haven't ever told anyone this," he says. "It's not really a story."

"Well, I want to know what happens. Did you shoot him in the leg?"

"Yes," Cliff says. He curls his lips around his teeth again.

"You shot him in the leg."

I defrost Cliff from old photos I've seen of his childhood. He's in a gold-colored soccer jersey and he's grinning, smashing his eyes to slits, a front tooth cockeyed, his cowlicks untamed. I try to add a gun to the visual.

"I shot him in the leg. He picked up the gun and handed it to me then he turned around. I got him in the back of the calf." Cliff hunches his shoulders. I'm about to ask what it felt like, that moment the metal hit skin. But before I can ask, Cliff jerks the wheel to the right to take a turn. "Is this what we're looking for?" he asks. Indeed, a green sign points the way. The car flies over a series of potholes, causing us both to jolt forward.

"Slow down," I say.

"No kidding," he says. "Anyway. Shane wanted me to touch his bleeding calf. He grabbed my hand. I resisted. He just kept staring at me, like in a creepy way, romantic, sort of, like he was going to lean in. And he was holding my hand. So finally, I took a rock and punched him with it."

I can tell this is the part of the story, more than the gun, more than the creepy staring, that Cliff doesn't like telling. One side of his face looks cramped.

"Shane didn't do anything. He just let go and covered his eye. I walked back to the bus stop. I had no money so I had to beg my way on." Cliff takes another mint. The hollows happen. An ancient van looms in front of us and Cliff slows the car. Someone has written *bite me you cougar* in the dirt on the back window.

"My mom broke up with Ray. She said he drank too much. And that was the end of Shane. We never saw each other again."

"I wonder what he's doing now," I say. Cliff shrugs. "Do you think he remembers it?"

"Sure," Cliff says. "Wouldn't you?"

And it's true that these are the things you hold onto.

"How come you've never told me that?" I ask.

"It's not the kind of thing you tell," he says. I take my thumb and run it over the prickly hair on his neck.

"It's not such a bad story," I say.

"You got worse?" he says. I run my thumb over his neck again. "Bite me you cougar," Cliff says.

"Do you know the story about the sibyl in the bottle?" I ask. Cliff squints. He shakes his head.

I tell him about her, about how Apollo wants her then traps her.

We sit quietly feeling each turn of the car. The fall has frozen the air. It has that particular quality of cool; it mutes the trees. Even the bark looks grayer.

"That's a sad story," Cliff says.

"There are a lot of sad stories," I say.

"Why didn't she just sleep with him?" Cliff asks. "He's the sexiest god, right?" I roll the bottle back and forth with my toe. "What's one thing I don't know about you?" he asks.

I'm not as good at things like this. The only memory I have, the only one that fits this game, is one I don't feel like telling.

"I used to step on ants outside and then try to heal them with Children's Tylenol," I say.

"That's it?"

"I once let a whole jar full of grasshoppers go in the living room."

Cliff shakes his head. "I'm never telling you anything again," he says. A fly lands on the side window.

"Okay, I know something. I had a Spanish teacher in high school, Mr. Fortelli, who used to always threaten to give me a bad grade. He said I was too quiet."

"Hard to believe."

"My friend Kelsie said to go and talk to him. She said if you went to talk with him, he'd be reasonable. Kelsie was an awful student, but she always got As in Spanish. Kelsie also had a big rack, to use your poetic phrasing."

Cliff smirks and brushes his eye with his hand. One eyebrow sticks up, pointing to the dotted roof of the car.

"She was stacked," I say.

"I get it," Cliff says.

"But she was plain and none of the guys really liked her. So anyways, I walked up to the door and the first thing I saw was Kelsie and Mr. Fortelli in the corner near the map of Mexico. Then I saw that the map of Mexico was weirdly crinkled."

"Uh oh."

"Mr. Fortelli had both hands up her shirt. Kelsie was sealed to the map, going up and down with his hands. And she saw me."

"What a perv."

"I backed up and waited for her around the corner. I said we should go to the principal. That year we had a new principal, a woman. I was excited to get Mr. Fortelli in trouble so I could avoid a C in Spanish."

"That's why I love you. Always thinking of others."

"But Kelsie said that if I told anyone, she would never speak to me again. To this day, I've never seen anyone so certain, so—I don't know—possessed. She looked like this." I point to the lunging animal on the bag of chips. "Years later, when we were both home for winter break, Kelsie told me that she lost her virginity to Mr. Fortelli on his daughter's bed."

"Gross," Cliff says.

"Yeah. She said she'd wished it would happen with him, and it had."

"She wished to lose her virginity on the Spanish teacher's daughter's bed?"

"I guess."

"So, what's the moral of your story?" Cliff asks.

"What's the moral of yours?"

Cliff shrugs. "Don't take the bus," he says.

"I never took another language class," I say. "Even in college. I stayed away."

"Is that the moral?"

"Does there have to be a moral?"

I roll down the window. Clouds are creeping in from the west. My sister, Kate, says that every year, people from the coasts go into the Rockies, the Sandias, the Jemez, and they don't know about flash-floods or lightning. They bring cheese and specialty bars wrapped in foil, then wham, they're dead. She told me this when she came to hike in these very mountains. It's as though, by acknowledging this, she avoids that fate.

Does knowing help? Sibyls are supposed to see into the future. Couldn't this one? When she said no to Apollo, she didn't see herself trapped in the bottle, wishing to die? Or was that *why* she didn't sleep with Apollo? Did she know that the outside world, from the captivity within glass would glow brighter and brighter? That because of the glass, the world inside of her would go vivid with longing and despair?

In the distance, I see a yellow stand of aspens, but the car turns into some thick juniper and cottonwoods and they disappear.

"Do you think he wanted to put something in or get something out?" I ask.

"What?"

"Do you think the point was to make a scar or to let something out, through the skin. You know, like bloodletting."

"Shane?" Cliff moves his head slowly in a no. "I couldn't tell you."

The wine bottle rolls under the seat and hits something metal.

"If Apollo gave you one wish, what would you wish for?" I ask.

"To not have to sleep with Apollo," Cliff says.

"I might wish for a baby."

Cliff looks at me sideways. "It would come out half-god," he says.

"It would come out, though."

"Yes," he says. "I suppose so. But maybe through the crown of your head."

"A baby for every grain of sand."

"A baby for every turning tree," he says, "and you would be one busy woman."

And then there they are, yellow as a room of canaries. This is what they do at the end of their season—yelp this color into the desert sky, then send it scattering to the red ground. Cliff parks the car under a stand of them. I open the door.

"Look at that," Cliff says, pointing to a rainstorm of leaves sent sailing with a wind. His brow has relaxed. In typical desert fashion, the blue sky of the morning has transformed to dark clouds. There will be storms tonight. The trees will go silver with winter.

Cliff's mom told me about a client once, a fourteen-year-old girl dying of leukemia. I was sitting on the sofa after brunch, stuffed to the gills, watching a cartoon and she just told me, out of the blue. All this girl wanted was for a particular boy to come to her bedside. She talked of nothing else. But when the girl's friends finally dragged the boy there, the girl wouldn't look at him.

She was embarrassed about the state of her skin. Then she died. Connie finished this story, slapped her thighs, and got up to clean some counters.

Cliff arches his back. "Let's walk," he says.

"It's going to storm."

"I know," he says. Far off over another set of hills, the first lightning flashes. The wind moves slowly. The world seems to shiver under its big hand. Families in colorful jackets pack their cars, fleeing the mountains.

Cliff closes his door, but I wait, caught for a moment.

Injuries and scars. I do have them. I was ten when Derrick arrived. My father had just left us—a trial separation everyone knew would last. My mother needed a project. Derrick was a foster kid, fourteen, skinny and big-eyed. He'd been beaten up at the group home, probably because of his willowy build, the way his hands tapered like a girl's. My mother set him up in our guest room on a borrowed bed with striped sheets, the room that used to be my father's study.

In the first weeks, Derrick drew into himself like a sea-snail snatched from its rock. And his silence lured out of my mother a warm, maternal heat. "How was school?" she'd ask him, in a way that she never asked me, her eyes damp and curious, her mouth parted in anticipation. He'd mumble fine, and try and walk away, but she'd try harder, following him with questions about his homework, his school supplies, sports, and friends. She urged me to sit next to him at dinner, to ask him to go swimming at the Y. She assigned the two of us chores to do in tandem—planting a berry patch out back, reorganizing the pots beneath the stove. When he wasn't around, she asked me my opinion. How did I think he was doing? Did he say anything to me about being happy or sad?

It makes sense to me now. She wasn't playing favorites. She was trying to make up for the world's bad temper.

Derrick stayed away from me as much as he could. He understood that he was treading on someone else's turf. If I came in to talk to my mother while the two of them watched television, he'd get up and go to his room.

My mother tried and tried. She bought him new shirts, the baggy shorts all the boys were wearing, even a skateboard. But she couldn't quite get him to relax. He ate his meals quietly and rinsed his plate. He kept all his clothes neatly stacked in the drawers, his duffle bag folded atop the dresser. It was as if he expected, at any moment, to have to leave.

One Saturday, maybe a few months after he'd arrived, she told me she wanted to take him on a field trip, just the two of them, out to the lake. Nature might do him good. I'd understand, right? I went to my friend Jenny's house, but I remember the feeling clearly, like my insides were being peeled away, leaving all my nerves exposed. I was a ringing thing, a bell chiming out into a windy sky. Jenny left me in her bedroom, confused by my unwillingness to play any of the games she suggested, and I quietly ripped the tail off a stuffed squirrel near her bed.

That night, my mother tucked me in. I tried to tell her about it, that I didn't feel well. "You'll survive, sweetie," she said, and patted my head. "You're a very fortunate child."

It began again, the feeling of being a bell in a big wind. I wanted my mother. I wanted my father. I wanted them both back, and to myself. I waited until I heard her close the door to her bathroom, turn on the faucet, open a drawer. The tile was cold under my feet.

"What's wrong?" she asked. Her mouth was bare of lipstick, flecked with the faintest white toothpaste.

I could have said that I missed her. That I missed my dad. I'm sure I weighed the response my honesty would get—that quick brush of her hand over my hair. So instead, I thought of what we learned in school, about bad touching, what to tell and when.

I twisted my hands together and told her a story. I watched her face contract, then loosen into a surface as smooth as a plate.

"What?" she asked.

My mother knelt down, staring into my eyes. "Are you telling me the truth?" she asked. I nodded. She tucked my hair away from my cheek. "Did he hurt you?" she asked. The words emerged from her as though they were locked in capsules of air. I shook my head. She kept her hand on my cheek. She closed her eyes and placed a knuckle against her furrowed brow, grinding it there. Then she reached out and held me to her, smoothing the back of my head.

"I'm sorry," she said. "My baby, my baby."

Derrick was gone the next morning. Drawers and closet empty, borrowed bed turned on its side.

My mother returned to me. I got her back. But she came with a ghost. In twenty-four years, we've never uttered his name—as if we can make him disappear from our past. As if by acting like the world can't hurt us, we will make it so.

I'm still in the car. A roll of thunder, then a clap. The noise happens once in the sky, then silently with feeling through the earth. I open the door, stand in the cool wind. I didn't bring a raincoat and within seconds, the shoulders of my shirt are soaked through. Cliff's hair is flat against his skull. He looks out into the gray and red, into the yellow and silver.

The rain is loud, falling against the wood, the dirt, the trees, my face. When drops hit the dusty trail, they stay risen like tiny bunkers.

Cliff's walking away from me, down into the trees. His body's small against the bleak view of peaks and I feel a wash of gratitude—for him, for the air and trees. A clump of leaves lands near my foot, layers of yellow and brown. I grab a handful and squeeze.

The truth is, if I had one wish right now, if I could wish on a handful of leaves—for baby Josephina, eternal life, eternal youth, domestic peace, a love that would never stray from me, never end—well, I've listened closely. I know what happens.

I wouldn't wish for anything at all.

I drop the leaves and lock the door. Cliff gets smaller and smaller. And then I follow him down the dust paths turning to mud, into the brown, silver and yellow, into the crashing storm.

ARS
PARENTIS

My father sits in his kitchen, head in hand. He looks out at the trees, wet with rain, covered in lichen and moss. The world outside is gray and green, shining like a gun.

"I don't think it can be fixed," he says. "Eloise and I are just very different people."

Last night, Eloise dragged my father out dancing. She wore a purple flapper dress and a headband low over her brow, long plastic white earrings and violet stockings. She is fifty-seven years old but "well-preserved," to use my father's parlance.

Some of my father's herring in cream sauce has fallen onto the table. Slowly, under the heat of the lamp, the congealed cream melts slightly, and the oil runs out of it.

I no longer clean anything in this house. I'm running an experiment. How dirty will it get if I do nothing about it? It isn't my house, after all. It hasn't been my house for more than half my life.

A box of newspapers has been sitting in the corner for years. Empty bottles of olive oil and Scotch litter the counter, gathering a gummy dust. Boxes of crackers from Costco, still bound together in their cellophane wrapping, form a barricade to the fruit bowl where several elderly potatoes turn green. Most of the bulbs in the light fixtures have burned out. This morning, I picked up a plate and it cracked in half along an old fissure. I've pointed this out, but he just shrugs. I don't understand why he doesn't see it, but he appears not to.

I used to try and fix things. I threw my purse down decisively and sank to my knees, cleaning, scrubbing, organizing. Then I'd grow angry. Or, more precisely, I'd wipe dust off the little painted cow in the kitchen and notice a hardening in my muscles, as if they were crystallizing. I could usually push my way past this. But then I'd feel a warming. And this warming would grow uncomfortable and—snap! That stupid little cow's painted eyes would look at me calmly, and I'd miss my mother but also hate her for dying, for leaving me here, for leaving me with this mess. Me, the only child, the end of the line. And then my father would go to use the phone book and the pristine kitchen shelf would be a disaster again: tipped over picture frames, fallen cow, wrinkled piles of bills, a half-eaten dog bone. A thing inside me would frantically spin around and I'd start to cry, retreating to the old bedroom so that I wouldn't start to yell.

Who can spend time this way, in a loop like that?

I happen to like Eloise. My mother has been dead a long time now. Her bones, if they're still there in the pine box, are likely some version of white now, clean of all that weighed them down. I don't know where she is, the actual woman with her penchant for sparkly jewelry and plain meals, her actual energetic presence. I don't know if she is gone, ghost, or something else. Every once in a while, I almost feel her, peering in on me, though less and less and less.

My father has lost most of his hair. The skin around his eyes looks thin and puffed. Metal pieces have replaced several of his human parts. He takes pills for things he won't tell me about. But every morning he walks his dogs up the mountain. Every night he drinks expensive wine. He's bedded several women, maybe more than several, in the years since my mother died. Occasionally, if I do laundry, I find colorful lacy underwear mixed in with the stained towels. He keeps KY Jelly in various drawers, including the drawer with the screwdrivers and nails.

I'm aging too. If you read anything at all, it will tell you, somehow, overtly or covertly, that my job on the planet was to marry and reproduce. If you read anything recent, it will suggest I do this while also being brilliant and socially valuable in my career. On the other side of thirty-five now, I don't have children or a spouse. My career has legs, but not long thin ones. I write a medical newsletter and marketing copy for a large insurer. Once robust, literally filled with promise, my eggs now (according to all of the reading material) grow daily less round, less likely to promise anything other than heartache. Men I date understand this on a rational level, but don't actually understand it—the depth of existential panic, the longing.

Less and less and less. I can't sleep at night and sometimes I stay awake and I look at pictures of men on the sperm bank websites. I consider having their baby, except it's frowned upon to say that. I would just be having my own baby, but with half of their genes. The bank promises me these men have excellent genes. The bank accepts only one percent of applicants, those with no family history of cancer or mental illness. The men have strong hearts and high IQs and they do things like play blues guitar and hike with their families.

"You and Eloise are very different people, but everyone is different from everyone," I say to my father. "You were also different from Mom."

My father, a physician, never says, "yes but I loved your mother," though he could. He refrains from incriminating statements, from half-truths or blazing truths. I know he did love my mother, and even if he couldn't say it then, he could say it now. Love gets easier in retrospect. It turns homogenous and kind, tinged with memory-honey. He might now paint a tableau of them holding hands, kissing one another's fingers while a sun set over a silver sea. In the moment, though, their love fussed like static on an old television, all its dots fierce and noisy. My mother was sick and dying. My father had an eye trained on exit routes. My mother took pills that numbed her mind and made her stand in front of the refrigerator scooping peanut butter out with her fingers. My father once, tired of watching this, poured tabasco into the canister. This is a kind of attachment. This is someone's version of love.

Last night at the party at the hospital where my father works, Eloise had several glasses of wine while my father sipped one. Hers: white and sparkly.

His: Reserve Pinot Noir from the Willamette Valley. Swing music blared from the bandstand. Eloise reached out an arm to my father.

Let us stop for a moment to appreciate the arm of Eloise: muscular and well-formed. It has none of the thickening of most other fifty-something women. Before her husband died, Eloise worked as a pharmacist. But, she decided, she wanted to prevent people from getting sick, not medicate them, so now she teaches Pilates and yoga in a converted post office. Eloise can do handstands and then fall back over her legs elegantly, as if her midsection were nothing but air.

Eloise never paints her nails. She, unlike my carefully manicured and made-up mother, wears no make-up beyond a brush of mascara. She keeps her dark curls oiled and cut close to her head. Tidy and efficient, Eloise can dance. My father does not dance. At the party, he clutched his wine glass as if it were a parking brake.

I don't know any of this, of course. I wasn't there. This was the story told by my father, imagined by me.

My father clutched his wine glass and Eloise grabbed his fleshier arm and she tugged him and he locked his metal knees, his metal hip. He would not budge.

Eloise tried to tug again.

"Knock it off," my father said.

Eloise made pursed kissy lips and batted her lightly mascaraed lashes. She began to wiggle her hips. She waved her muscular arms in front of her. Bait on a hook. A carrot dangled to a hungry horse. Only my father felt no hunger, or at least was not a horse. Eloise took another glass of sparkly white wine and tipped the whole thing down her throat. My father hardened his eyes. Eloise shrugged her shoulders.

She turned to the man next to my father, an endocrinologist who'd never married. She shimmied at him, extended her long, shapely arm. The endocrinologist turned to my father who remained locked up. The endocrinologist turned back to Eloise and held out his hand.

The endocrinologist, a very short man with pungent breath, and Eloise. Eloise and the endocrinologist.

He moved his awkward body and she used him the way a cat might use a tree. She threw a leg around him and arched back, she arched forward, she ran her hands along his trunk. She pressed her small bosom to his suited-up chest. She tipped her head back and tried to catch my father's eye, tried to wink and beckon, but my father had left the party.

And now Eloise has not called him and he has not called Eloise.

"I just hate living my life alone," he says.

"You have me," I say. I'm usually in California, but my father doesn't point this out. He scratches his knee. The dog whines from the other room.

"It's bad to sit here inside like this. Let's go for a walk," I say. My father stares at the wall, at a hanging print of a range of mountains. He looks at the trim of the window. What does he see? And then he gets up and gets his shoes and puts them on, and I go and look for mine.

It's the house I grew up in. My bedroom sits at the end of the long hall, the pink drapes blocking out natural light. Years ago, I unscrewed the light fixture from the ceiling to use it in a rental, and now the bulbs glare down, unadorned, creating little orbs of light on the wood. I brought almost nothing with me this weekend, figuring I could scrounge enough from the old dresser to wear if I needed to. But little remains to scrounge. Just a few moth-eaten sweaters and Girl Scout sashes, a pair of terrible sweat pants and uncomfortable rhinestone T-shirts, saved from my adolescence without reason. By my bed, though, sits the old, wooden cigar box filled with odds and ends—old earrings, glass bracelets, and a small zippered pouch filled with my mother's junk jewelry. I always look through it, a little ritual each time I visit. I take out the pieces, look at their broken bits, and put them all back. But today, I feel like pinning her to my chest, and so I choose a pin I bought her once for her birthday, a silver sun.

We set out in his car, his dog Rennie, in the back seat, panting out air that smells like dying earthworms. It's not yet noon. The fir trees point at the cloudy sky, like arrows sent up from the center of the earth. The stereo broke years ago, and so we listen to rubber on asphalt.

Here we are. Three animals in a metal capsule hurtling across a forest on a strip of manmade rock. We'll emerge from the capsule and tie the different species to a rope, appreciating and then condemning the verve with which he embraces odors, movements, grass. We'll trudge up a mountain, a novelty, because we don't trudge in forests much anymore, this species to which I belong.

My father has never once asked me about children, never pressured me. And still, it remains a fact. He produced me. He handed me the torch. And I plunged it into icy water.

What does it matter? So many people are busy in bed, busy in labor, busy pouring ideas into the heads of small people.

My father's cell phone chirps.

"Are you going to get that?" He glances down at it, sitting in the dirty well of his parking break.

"You get it," he says. It is, of course, Eloise.

"Hello?" I say.

"Oh, hello, Ramona," she says. And then with worry in her voice, "Is this Ramona?"

"Yes, yes," I say.

"I was calling your father, is he busy?"

"Tell her I'm driving," he says.

"Oh, he's driving," she says.

"Tell her I will talk to her when I talk to her," he says.

"What does that mean?" she says.

"Dad," I say. "Want me to hold the phone like this?" I hold it to his ear but he bats it away.

"Can you tell him that we need to talk about this?" says Eloise.

"Dad, Eloise wants to talk about this."

"Will you tell him that I have to go teach my yoga class at two, but I would like to discuss this with him before I go, because I have that dinner tonight at Chris's and I don't want to go through the whole day like this."

"Hang on a sec," I say. I translate this for my father. He keeps his face locked on the road.

"We're about to go for a walk," I say. "Up the mountain." She doesn't say anything.

"Do you want to come with us?" I ask.

My father stomps off into a meadow with proud, hyper Rennie. Rennie lifts his leg high and fast, urinates in a life-affirming spray, then lowers his haunches to do his other business. My father turns his head out of deference and respect.

Efficient Eloise arrives quickly in her old yellow Miat, sporting khaki outdoor pants and a fluffy moss green fleece. Small gold ball earrings clutch at her lobes. She looks, as she always looks, freshly laundered.

"Hello, Phil," Eloise says. Much shorter than my father, she tips her head to see him. Rose petals float on the white ponds of her cheeks. Her eyebrows arch like moth wings.

I look away, down at some daisies that have sprouted in the grass. I stoop down to pick one, and Rennie thinks I'm crouching to pet him. He leaps, spry, and licks my cheek.

"I don't want to be fighting," Eloise says. She reaches her hand out to my father. He doesn't take it. Her fingers land on the cuff of his coat. They could be a child's fingers, the way they try to find purchase. My father moves his arm away.

"I want to walk my dog," he says.

"Is this about the dancing?" she asks.

"Come on, Rennie," my father says. Rennie bounds back to him. I stand up. My father starts to trudge.

Eloise turns to me, eyes shining.

Eloise's husband died in a cycling accident. They were in Italy, touring the wine regions. He'd just had mussels in a saffron broth, and mussels always made him ill. They'd argued about that. And then he got run over by a bus. Five years ago.

"Dad," I say. He turns to me. His eyes look urgent.

"Where are you going?" I ask.

"Phil," Eloise says, her voice wavering. I can feel my father stiffen from here.

At that moment, a chipmunk races across the trail and Rennie springs to life. My father has the leash in his hand, and one leg rests on a slick bit of trail near a tree root. Something happens—the yanking, the slick trail, and my father cries out as he wobbles on one leg, then topples.

Eloise screams.

"Shut up," cries my dad, trying to get up.

"Eloise!" I say. "Dad!"

"Get the fucking dog!" he yells. And I see the whippet, a fawn colored blur in a stand of trees. I run after him.

"Rennie! Rennie, come!"

What movies have a girl running like this through the woods, as if she were pursued, only actually she is the pursuer? I think this as I run. I don't feel totally within my body. The sensation, like running next to myself. I can feel my knees catch my bones just a second after they actually do that.

The dog stops beneath a tree, throws his front paws up on it. He barks and barks. I can still hear Eloise screaming, though she is not screaming anymore. But that scream did not come from this moment of time. I'm sure that scream was attached to another scream, a scream in Italy, or even before that.

My hand on the dog's neck, groping for the leash, then the dog's face smiling up at me.

My mother went into labor early, and then I didn't come out. They sliced her up trying to get to me, and she bled and bled and never recovered fully. She suffered from residual pain all of her life. She told me this many times, and maybe it's part of the reason I'm here in the woods with a dog and a father and nothing else in the winter of my thirty-ninth year.

When I get back to the trail, I can see Eloise and my father in the parking lot. My father holds onto Eloise's shoulders. She unlocks the passenger door of her Miata.

"Take the dog home," my father says to me as I approach. He hands me his keys.

"Are you okay?" I ask.

"I'll take him to the hospital," Eloise says. "He's fine but he might need X-rays." She has raised her chin and lowered her lids. She looks proprietary, but I leave it be.

Rennie turns around three times on the seat then lies down. He licks the bottom of his paw. He licks and licks and licks, then starts to chew with a manic intensity, like he wants to find out what's inside. I flick him on the forehead. Then he groans and settles his chin on the seat. The gravel in the lot gives way to the broken asphalt of the country road. On one side, a small farm with corn and cherries and beans. My mother used to stop there and chat up the farmer. Once, she bought me these little cornhusk dolls. I loved their flat bodies and bizarre red felt pinafores, but eventually the husks turned brittle and flaked away.

We pull out onto the real road. The sun brooch falls off its pin backing, slides down my chest and lands between the seat and brake. I reach my hand to get it and the car swerves dangerously toward another car. The driver honks and flips me off and I accidentally pass the turnoff for my father's house. When I finally stop at a stoplight, I feel something like strobe lights flashing inside my brain.

My mother's bones rest in a Jewish part of the cemetery at the bottom of this hill. I've never visited her grave. Eloise's husband rests somewhere nearby. I wonder if they know each other. The thought contains an element of realism. As if they're friends somewhere, in a different realm, like Florida. I had dreams like this for years—that she had not died, that she had only lied to me about dying, instead enjoying a new life, a tackier life, but she felt good about it.

"You stupid fucking cunt!" the guy I almost hit yells.

I roll down my window, the strobe lights still going strong, my mother sitting in Florida with the husband who is now eternally sick from his mussels and she laughs and holds her brooch and I open my mouth to say something horrible back at him, *I hope your tiny dick falls off*, but he roars off, the lights green, and the guy behind me honks.

They're not in the emergency room. I suppose I should have known that when a doctor comes into the hospital, he wouldn't have to wait. I ask at the desk. Dr. Molan's daughter, I say. The receptionist taps her keys. A nurse disappears behind the swinging doors, and then returns. We go down the linoleum hallway into a curtained-off room. Eloise has taken off her fleece jacket, beneath which she wears a silky tank top. She fusses with the pillow behind my dad's head.

He opens his eyes and Eloise, upon seeing me, returns to her chair.

"Did you take the dog home?" my father asks.

"He's in the car."

"I told you to take him home."

"I'm going to get some 7Up," says Eloise.

"Take the dog home," my father says.

"Do you want anything?" I ask.

"They have to do an X-ray," he says. "I'll be out of here in a couple of hours."

I pick up his hiking pants from the stool nearby, caked with mud.

"I can clean these," I say. "Do you want me to go home and get you another pair?" He glances at the IV which they've set up to rehydrate him.

"Take the dog home," he says. "Stop screwing around with the rest of it."

In the hall, Eloise talks to a young male nurse. She gestures with one arm, swinging it in a port de bras, and in the other hand has a can of 7Up and two little cups. She sees me out of the corner of her eye. She raises the cups as if to signal me to stop. But I don't feel like stopping.

Who is Eloise? What do I really know about her? She came from a line and produced a line, but she'll always just be somebody else's family. I gesture to the elevator and move past.

I can see myself wavy and hazy in the outside of the elevator doors. I entered this hospital for the first time inside of my mother. We sat in a wheelchair, a helium balloon tied to its handle. Me, swaddled, held close, intoxicated by the new air and the dizzying scent of my mother's skin. My father behind her, wheeling us out. And then she entered it one awful day many years ago, barely able to breathe from pain, and I left motherless. One of these days, I'll bring my father here and will leave alone for good. Triangle to line to dot. They are just very different people, my father and Eloise. But we are not.

My father worked at this hospital. He took me here when I was small, let me sit in the nurse's station, eating lemon drops, banging all their knees with rubber mallets. I remember him then, busy and young, his thick dark hair waving across his brow. He wore collared shirts with patterned ties and when I grew sleepy, he'd pick me up and I would run a finger around the paisleys, the snowflakes, the flying birds. "This is my daughter," he would say, pressing a hand to my head.

I turn away from the opening doors. I should wait. I'm the family. I'll drive my father back up the hill, back to the mess of a house. My mother would have swiped the newspapers into the recycling with the side of her arm. She would have thrown the old food away, clucking softly, put bones in a pot for a chicken soup, boiled egg noodles, cleaned the grit from the cupboards with a cut up old tee-shirt. "You are a hopeless slob," she'd have said to my father, her face retaining its essential softness.

In our tiny bit of history, we did things this way. I can do all of that still.

"Excuse me," says a nurse, halting my progress. "Can I help you?"

"My father's in there," I say.

"His name, please?"

She types it into the computer, then breathes big and leads the way, her blue uniform flapping. She slides the curtain open.

"Oh, I think they went to X-ray," she says.

She points a finger down the hall. "You can probably catch them."

I walk out, down the hall, my steps getting faster until I'm running. And then my mother stands in an unfamiliar bedroom in front of an unmade bed, alone. She has no brooch. She waits, has been waiting. Her face looks very pale, but her eyes retain their intricate candle-like lights. She opens her mouth to speak. And then I see him in a wheelchair with one leg out straight, waiting for an elevator. Eloise stands beside him. The light in the hallway bangs brightly against the elevator doors, like a sun blasting down toward the silver sea. I stop running.

My father's head tilts toward Eloise's hip. She gently touches the top of his head, her fingers weaving through the remnants of his hair. He says something to her that makes her laugh. He reaches for her hand.

WHAT
TO EXPECT

Three a.m., four a.m., the inky blot of time between night and dawn, she sat up in bed covered in sweat. She couldn't blame her dreams. She'd stopped dreaming, as if her body knew she no longer needed to dream, that she'd stepped into a reality more surreal.

The baby could be born sickly, autistic. The baby could have a congenital defect, faulty DNA. The baby could have a less articulate problem—could be mean or exhausting or ugly. Really, this baby could be anybody.

The donor Emily picked was of Italian descent with "thick, dark hair and a lean, athletic build." He went to an Ivy League college before getting a law degree. When she added him to her list of favorites, an alert came up warning of limited and low supply. She clicked the question mark, and a small box informed her that if she wanted to use this donor, she should purchase as many vials as she thought necessary to "achieve her family planning goals." The next day, he had only half as many vials left and she felt a proprietary urge, a sweep of impulse. She purchased them, all eight for $425 apiece, in the same amount of time it might have taken her to snag a sweater at a sample sale.

A miracle, at thirty-nine, to get pregnant on the first try. But it happened. She had the vials shipped to a clinic, went to the clinic mid-cycle, and two weeks later missed her period. And now, thirteen weeks in, she felt seasick and stuffed, as though she'd eaten a loaf of white bread dipped in melted butter, as if she'd swallowed those expanding sponges. In line at the grocery store, in the car on the way to the pool, in the bed, at the editing studio—she was sick, she felt sick, so sick.

But no matter how bad she felt during the day, the bad feelings reached an apex at three a.m., when she sat up and felt like reaching inside herself and yanking her own uterus out. Who was she? Why had she done this? Wasn't it difficult enough to just be her, alone? Who was this baby? Whose DNA did he have? Whose history had she become inextricably bound up with?

Also, at three a.m., she felt broke. She felt broke because she was broke. She edited documentary films freelance, and even though she'd moved to Portland from San Francisco a year ago to cut her costs, given up the jewel-hued sunlight and bustling vibrancy of the Mission and lived in a small one-bedroom apartment with an oven the size of a milk crate and drove a ten-year-old car, even though she wore the same jeans she'd worn for four years, the sweaters with the holes under the arms, she hadn't been able to save more than two thousand dollars. She couldn't afford to have a special needs baby. The baby had to come out with a job or a trust fund. A tiny little stockbroker, a real estate developer, a nuclear scientist. Or perhaps it had to come out clutching the hand of its father, the Ivy League lawyer, a man sliding out after the infant, covered in that same grayish slime. She imagines the way a briefcase would feel against her most private parts as it edged its way into the world.

Also, it felt hot in the apartment in the middle of the night. No air conditioning. Bad ventilation in these old turn-of-the-century buildings. A smell sometimes flooded the place—orange mixed with vinegar, a bad, wrong smell, and she wondered if she lived above some kind of Superfund site—despite the hipsters and organic food, this city was full of them, and if the baby would not be born autistic but rather half tadpole or salamander. When she got up from bed to change her nightgown she'd catch a glimpse of herself in the mirror, the first hint of new fat coming into her arms and face, and she fought off the sense that she was no longer female in the way she used to be, but biological, a biological container, a device to transport a body. *Maternal.* It felt impossible to imagine that she'd ever escape this new identity. Still alone, if not exactly "single" with an infant in tow, she'd be in a category beyond romantic love. Used up. Right about then, the tiny mice with frozen feet went scampering down her spine.

Usually, morning brought with it a dose of reason. She had, after all, done this to herself. She paid quite a lot of money, in fact, to do this, and she was lucky that it worked. Congratulations, wrote the sperm bank. She wanted this baby. She wanted to be a mother. She didn't have forever to do this, to achieve her family planning goals. She could feel the solid weight of an infant in her arms, smell the soapy odor of its scalp. But more than all that, she could feel a new kind of tenderness, still a bit of an abstraction, but edging closer. Hard to name. But true, nonetheless. The entry ticket to her gender: a tenderness in the way that she touched even the kitchen sink, a kind of weak-kneed oozing love.

Emily spent hours in her editing studio, ostensibly working, but really surfing the chat room the sperm bank launched for its Donor 3431 consumers. She never posted. But she could lurk around the Donor 3431 messages and read about the successes his sperm had produced.

"A beautiful curly-headed boy."

"We have two 3431 boys! Both times insemination happened quickly, and they are super healthy kids! The only problem is that one has a seafood allergy!"

"3431 blessed me with a little girl, Jamaica May, completely perfect in every way."

And a woman from Lake Oswego named Belle posted, asking for a few more vials so she could try for a biological sibling for her daughter.

Emily's most recent credit card statement took her breath away. She'd not paid off the vials, or the acupuncture, or the supplements she bought at the fancy vitamin store, or the ridiculous designer maternity jeans Mariette insisted she buy so she'd feel pretty all the way to the end, the water purifier, the utility bills they let her charge, a speeding ticket. She reread the woman's post. 3431 had retired, the DNA gone, the last vials in other 3431 mother's—or aspiring mothers'—possession.

"Hi Belle, I have seven extra vials." She had to do it. She didn't need them. It was goodhearted. And also, they cost $425 a vial—she needed that cash.

She'd not expected that the woman, Belle, would write back so fast—her email in blue with a happy face at the end. She'd not expected the transaction to occur that week. She'd expected, or at least expected in retrospect, to receive a check by mail, fax some release forms and send Belle to the clinic to pick up the vials. But Belle wanted to give her the money face-to-face, to meet another mother of a 3431. She offered to pay more than the $425 a vial that Emily had paid, more than the premium Emily had asked for. She offered $600 a vial. From one 3431 to another, she wrote. You're a saving grace, she wrote, a miracle worker!!!

Belle didn't say she would be coming with her husband, but she did. She showed up on a Friday afternoon dressed in white pants and a bright turquoise sweatshirt, her ponytail as slick as saran wrap. She talked fast with an animated face, the whole of her iris visible. Crazy eyes, Emily thought. She wondered if their baby had the same eyes. The baby was with Belle's sister, Belle explained. "We weren't sure if it would be weird for you. You know, to meet a sibling of your baby before you meet your own."

The husband didn't match the wife. He wore a faded T-shirt and Converse high tops. His limbs were long, slack, and he hadn't shaved. His sperm obviously didn't work.

"So, you're doing this solo?" said Belle. Her lipstick might have been called cotton candy or bubble gum. So very pink, like the most private scar.

"Yes," Emily said.

"That's so brave. I admire you. I don't know if I would have the cojones."

The man looked up at Emily suddenly, and then at his wife. He smiled with his mouth tucked in. He had gray eyes, the color of a cat's fur, and tiny glints of blond stubble on his face, though his hair had gone mostly salt and pepper.

"It's crazy you're just right here in Southeast. I mean, I knew there'd be other moms but I thought they'd be, oh, I don't know, like in Tennessee or Alaska."

"Yeah, well," Emily said. "I actually think there's a certain demographic buying most of the sperm. You know—Portland, San Francisco, Los Angeles. All our kids will probably be at Oberlin together in eighteen years."

The woman widened her eyes further. "I never really thought about that."

She smiled then, a conversation stopping smile. Emily got the consent forms out and handed them to Belle.

"Do you think I could use your restroom?" she finally said.

That animal sense that flared, alone with an attractive man. As if she still had a dance card to fill. His T-shirt looked as soft as the skin of a popped balloon.

"Cute apartment," the husband said. What had he said his name was? Evan, Emily thought. Or something like that. Maybe Elliot. "I manage a few of these buildings down here. Not this one, though."

"I used to manage apartments," Emily said. "I mean, one building. When I was younger. To get the free rent."

"Yeah, that's why I got into it, too. I was making films and it was an easy side job."

"You make films?" Emily asked, and she looked straight into his face, which sent a seizing heartbeat through her. He had front teeth that over-lapped slightly.

"I used to. Now I sell real estate."

"I edit films," Emily said.

Belle emerged from the bathroom.

"Emily edits films," the husband said. Belle smiled widely, her Lite-Brite eyes beneath rainbow-shaped brows.

"I'd love to keep in touch," she said, taking the vials. "Would you want to? Keep in touch? I know it's weird, but we're family now, in a way, and it might be nice to keep tabs on the babies. Learn a little about the gene pool. Of course, only if you want to. I mean, there's a whole online community for 3431s—but having one *literally* across town! It's pretty, well, I don't even know what to call it! Wacky."

No, thought Emily. Not wacky. Alarming. And, no, she didn't want that. She wanted to pretend this was an average situation, that she was not bring-ing a child into an insane circumstance, into a world peppered with sixty half-siblings. She'd not meant to live a life that kept resembling chaos and disorder, that always seemed to be a little undone. But this life kept arriving at her doorstep. And you had to let life in, however it arrived.

She looked at Evan/Elliot and she got a Post-it from her desk. She wrote out her phone number, retracing the number twice with her ballpoint before handing it over.

"It's going to be *fine*," Mariette said. "You just have to tell yourself that no thought that comes to you at three a.m. gets full consideration until you're sitting with a cup of coffee and a bowl of cereal with the radio on. Then it can try to get your attention." Thank God for Mariette. She did hair downtown, the most expensive hairdresser in Portland, she joked, though she used to do hair in LA. She used to charge as much for a haircut as she now paid in rent. But then she got pregnant by a famous married client, and he paid her to move away, tucking a bit of college money in a trust account for the kid. So, Mariette left, moved to Portland. She claimed that nothing about this situation bothered her, and Emily felt a kind of warm awe. Because it genuinely seemed true.

The world was crazy, Mariette said. You had to just make your own sense of things, because the rest was just the lace over the table. Mores, customs— just the lace over the table, you took it off and you had the table, the real thing.

The child, Poni, had sandy skin, disconcertingly blue eyes, and blond streaks in otherwise dark hair. She was going to be trouble, Mariette liked to say, proudly caressing her striped locks. Poni had a theatrical flair, too, one had to assume her father's. At three, she already threw seductive looks at anyone who gazed her way, tossing her arms out toward objects she wished to touch, lifting her legs high as she pranced across the floor.

The two women sat in Emily's living room, or the tiny alcove that served as the living room. Mariette wore a heavy perfume that smelled like incense.

"Maybe it's your diet," Mariette said. "Are you eating a lot of carbs? Bread and sugar? Because that can give you anxiety."

"No, I'm freaked out. What if the baby has a big disability? What will I do? And what if the baby is fine, but really colicky? I don't have anyone to help me. Why did I do this?" She pictured the woman, Belle, with her Saran Wrap hair and her too-attractive husband, their quiet nights in front of a television, walking an old golden retriever by the river, cooking lasagna, and bickering about chores and she began to cry. Mariette reached for Poni, who came and sat in her lap. "Why is she crying?" Poni asked.

"Because she is silly," Mariette said. "You really have to stop with this," Mariette said. "Because it's done. You did this and it's a marvelous blessing that it worked—your first try, incredible. It worked, and it's done. There's nothing in the bloodwork or your genetic history to suggest a disability. And you used that first-rate sperm—better sperm than the rest of us. You're just stressing yourself out. You're more likely to have a totally healthy baby that you upset with your anxiety and stress than anything else."

"Better sperm," said Poni.

"Oh great," said Mariette.

She wanted to cry harder, to lose herself in a spasm of tears, to wail and howl and beat on the floor pillows and throw a few of her belongings against the wall. But her phone started ringing. A number she didn't recognize. Just a second.

It was Elliot. He'd been thinking about her film editing. He'd been out of the business a while, and seeing her made him wonder if he could maybe get back in. He had some footage—old footage, but still. Maybe if she could send some of her films his way? He could take a look and see if they could work together? Did that seem too weird given the circumstances?

Of course, yes, sure, email, will do it later this afternoon.

Maybe we can have coffee and discuss if it's simpatico.

"What?" Mariette asked. "The guy whose wife bought all that sperm?" She raised her brows but said nothing.

"He said he liked the work," Emily said, a week later, at Mariette's. He also said that he wanted to get together—to discuss a possible partnership. He shot two hundred hours of footage in Kuala Lumpur a few years back and he thought if he had a good collaborator . . . . But she didn't tell Mariette that.

Mariette lived in a beautiful loft overlooking the Willamette River, the pewter water rushing so fast it looked still. Mariette folded laundry on her sleek leather sofa, drinking a mid-afternoon mimosa while Emily poked at a pile of almonds. Her insides had been lurching around for months, rising up and plunging down, wagging from side to side like a deranged squid— surprising her randomly with bouts of vomiting, even after days of peace. But now the feeling shifted. It felt more like an arrow of fire had burned away the water, the squid, and left in its wake, a scorched and shivery feeling.

Mariette put down a pair of tiny crimson pants and let her manicured hand rest atop them. She looked steadily at Emily, her long blond bangs hanging halfway over her eyes.

"You better think this one through," Mariette said.

You see you break through one cultural norm and you come out in a dizzying new world. Who's to say that if you impregnate yourself using a stranger's bio-logical refuse, his ejaculate, his sperm—if you put a stranger's sperm willingly into your own parts in the sterile and welcoming world of a clinic, if you say to the world, I do not need a man, and I do not need support, and I do not need approval, and I will do this alone, then who is to say you cannot eat steak with a toothpick in a fancy restaurant or catch your menstrual blood with a measuring cup and water the flowers with it? Who's to say you cannot eat cat or ride a goat or masturbate with an exhaust pipe while extracting your own teeth? Where's the line? And who's to say that you can't go to a drink at eight o'clock at night in the Hotel DeLuxe, sixteen weeks pregnant with the half-sibling of your date's child? You're walking a tightrope over something sure, but you were already on it. The only difference is that now you have company.

The pregnancy didn't yet show. Just a tightness and mild puffiness, easy enough to hide without really trying. She could still wear most of her dress-es. A green one with a ruched middle, a low-cut neckline that showcased the new heaviness in her breasts. A gold necklace and no earrings. Her hair down, no up, no down. Down, around her shoulders. Just a tiny bit of that floral perfume oil behind her knees.

The articles said to stay calm and relaxed, to eat a balanced diet, to avoid caffeine and anti-depressants and sleep medication and Advil. Listen to music, talk to the baby, go to prenatal yoga and massage, take your vitamins.

But who could say what this baby needed? Maybe this baby needed Emily to be held, to be touched, to have strong fingers take down her underwear and slide up inside of her, towards the baby, as if smoothing something out, as if two insertions might cancel each other's chaos and make calm again.

"You can have one glass of wine," he said. He ordered her a pinot grigio, tapping hard on the menu with his hand as if challenging the waiter to argue. "The French do it, and they have beautiful children." They sat in a corner booth, both of them sharing the curved vinyl bench. The walls had wood-paneling and dim light—restored old Portland glamor. She could feel his personness, a solid warmth on his skin, a kinetic charge in the air around him. They talked shop—film school, they talked San Francisco, Los Angeles, directors, Final Cut Pro. And then he mentioned his upbringing, so they talk parents (his father died when he was seven, hers when she was thirty. His mother lived in Santa Barbara. Hers had also died, but a long time ago. I'm so sorry, he said. Yes, thanks, she said. It's hard to be the last one standing.) She had one glass, and he asked if she wanted another. She shook her head and ordered a lemonade. You can sip from mine, he said, sliding his beer over to her—he liked a particular Oregon brew, Ninkasi lager. He was wry but attentive and they never mentioned the sperm, they never mentioned the woman, Belle. Three beers in, two hours at the bar and he looked at her gravely as she laughed and he leaned in and kissed her, his tongue soft and languid, his teeth knocking hers, his hands as strong as she imagined, down her low back, kneading her like a cat might, pressing his nose to her forehead. You smell familiar, he said, you smell so good. She had an impulse to say something sharp, to pull away and say, "I can't, aren't you married?" but a stronger one to let his hand continue to do that. Because what business, really, was it of hers? It was his business, and she didn't know the half of it—what drew people together, what broke them apart. She wasn't born yesterday—it had been nearly forty years, in fact, since she was born and she'd seen plenty of things happen. And no one had touched her like this in a year, in more than a year. Her body was doing so many things to her brain.

Do you want to get out of here, he asked. He could take her home since she walked over, and yes, sure, and they were in the apartment, in the bed within twenty minutes, all of their clothes tangled together with the dust bunnies and papers on the floor, they were making noises like the creaking of doors, like the slamming open of windows, and after he came inside of her they both laughed nervously. No need to worry, right? No need to worry.

God, she thought in the morning, waking alone in the messy room. God, god. She took the car, drove out to Target and spent a hundred and eighteen dollars on little plastic things—binkies and mobiles and diapers and a few bottles of lotions. And also a new razor for herself and a cheap but sexy lace slip. She handed the credit card over in a daze, signed the little screen with a fake pen. She sat in her car in the heat of the day, in the large oversized lot, four bags of crap on her lap, and thought: it is okay, is it okay? And for no reason she could exactly pinpoint, though not for no reasons certainly, she cried. Such tears, as if she'd been saving them in a bathtub inside of herself. She let go in the car, her head on the steering wheel, until she heard a rapping on her window and jolted up, her heart pounding, and a little old lady in a long blue coat asked her if she knew she was in a handicap spot.

"I don't want this second baby." He'd come over after his run, a pocket of unaccounted for time. "It wasn't my idea to do all of this."

He wasn't married to Belle. Emily sat by the large window and traced a line in some dust. Their fourth meeting. The first was the sperm sale. The second the Hotel DeLuxe. The third, five days ago—a walk by the river and then back to her apartment. And now this time, impromptu by text. Here he sat, a man with sad, absorbent eyes. She held his hand. He looked at her hard, his gaze so unfiltered it made things jump inside of her. His last name was Green, a lovely last name. Nothing about Elliot Green did not strike Emily as indefinitely lovely—someone she might have met back in Providence twenty years ago in college. The kind of man taken off the market quietly in his late twenties by a savvy young woman who understood far more about life and love than Emily had back then, some young woman that hedged her bets and secured her fate. Those men seemed abundant back in the day. She slept with them routinely, casting them aside whenever she felt suffocated or bored. And then, one day, years later—it seemed to happen suddenly—they began to disappear, endangered species brought down by a cataclysmic event. When one materialized, back from a year spent shooting a documentary overseas, back from the Peace Corps, or newly widowed or divorced, you had to claw your way over to him and try to be heard over the din of other women. But by then, he inevitably had his eyes set on a younger version of you—equally smart, equally talented, but ten years more fertile and lean. So, Elliot was rare—or his proximity felt rare—a beautiful, intelligent man who looked cast from nature's materials, uncorrupted by the mechanized, mediated world. She hadn't felt this kind of raw, unadulterated attraction to a man in so long; she hadn't expected to again.

"Have you told her what you're feeling?" Emily asked.

"Yes," he said. "But she thinks I'm just scared. Scared of loss, scared of committing again because of loss."

"Again?" she asked.

He'd been very happily married, he explained. To a woman named Joyce, for five years.

"You were married?" Emily asked.

"Yes," said Elliot.

"What happened?" Emily asked.

"She died," he said. He rubbed his temple and stared at the wall. She felt herself surge toward him as if she were trying to keep him from toppling over, her hands landed jerkily. She rubbed the edge of his flannel shirt. She moved them to his chest.

She died of cancer, he said, and Belle was her best friend through all of it. The night of Joyce's death he leapt in bed with Belle, both of them wild with grief and longing, both of them too scared to sleep alone. And he hadn't really tried very hard to get out of that bed during the dark months that followed. Then Belle wanted to get pregnant. She felt time slipping away. Look what happened to Joyce. Elliot couldn't commit, so she went ahead and did it without him, with donor sperm. They'd parted ways then, he said. Only when she needed him—she had a hard pregnancy—he'd returned, he'd stayed by her side. He and Belle did hard things together. This tether connected them, not love, exactly. Not happiness. But it sometimes felt deeper than happiness. Or at any rate, more permanent. Then the baby came, and it got complicated. Because he loved the baby. He'd never meant for it to get this way, but time passed. With Emily, now he felt this real thing, this happy, amazing thing for Emily that he didn't think he'd ever feel again after Joyce.

She felt like crying, only it didn't seem right. It didn't seem like her pain. She got up and got him a Ninkasi, which she'd taken to buying, to storing in the bottom of her fridge. He drank it, and then asked if she wanted to take a shower, and everything about it felt perfect to her, except a few notable details, of course.

"Looks great," said Dr. Lombardi. "Your vitals are all excellent. You're doing an excellent job. How do you feel?"

She felt marvelous, no longer sick. She felt radiant, like she wore a light bulb under her skin and Elliot switched it on. Or maybe the baby switched it on. "We can find out the sex in a week or two," said the doctor.

"It's going to be a boy," Emily said.

"Why do you say that?"

"The male sperm swim faster, thaw better. That's what I've heard."

"Well, you can't always fit into statistics," said the doctor. "Only time will tell."

Dr. Lombardi wore a big gold wedding band on her large hands. She had two daughters and a son, she said. Best things in her world. She didn't say anything about Emily doing it alone. No, "you are so brave," or "I'm glad for you that it's worked out," just quiet, efficient work. Emily was the patient, Dr. Lombardi the physician. A relationship as old as civilization. She kept it simple, reliable, straightforward. Emily could reach out and hug her. Why not do it? Who was to say she could not hug her doctor if she felt like it? But she didn't.

Elliot came almost every day—after his run, before heading home, and even sometimes late at night. He rubbed her back and they stayed up talking—about movies, mostly, but sometimes about books. He couldn't stay over, but they often pretended to sleep, and twice she fell asleep on his chest, only to wake up by herself, a raw, roaring feeling dancing lightly on her skin.

"I'm pregnant, too," Emily said to him. "You know that."

"But with you it's different," he had said. He moved his hand over the blue sheets and set them on Emily's growing belly. She felt them there for a while. Then she put her hands over his hands and kissed him. He kissed her back and pressed her to the sofa, took off her dress.

She felt it growing inside her—the swelling affection, the manic attention to his texts. He got near her and every cell in her body leapt. A baby grew inside of her, too, nurtured, she thought, by this twin affection. She carried a baby half related to Elliot's baby—and in some bizarre loop of logic, that meant she carried his baby. The world confounded. Once you removed the lace from the table, you still had the table. There were too many metaphors. Sometimes there were no metaphors for things. It was not like a table, it was just a man. Elliot Green. It was not something you could talk about. It was private, shocking, right.

"It's a girl," the ultrasound tech told her. Emily really and truly showed now, the curve like an exercise ball starting to rise out of her. Elliot never mentioned it. He ran his hand over it wordlessly.

"It's a girl," she told him. He didn't say anything and she watched his face, so still, his gaze on her skin.

"A girl," he finally said. "Congratulations."

She had a few projects, though not enough of them. She edited a local web commercial for an organic antibacterial spray. She edited some footage shot in Thailand for a friend's documentary. But she really spent the days in a state of enraptured waiting.

"I want to see your house sometime," she said, fingering his hair on the sofa in the sun. He brought over expensive crackers, a dense kind with tiny fig pieces in them, and a cheese without mold he knew she could eat. He brought over bars of chocolate, too, and fizzy fruit juices—always a different flavor. His head lay in her lap, against the baby.

"Belle said she was going to call you," he said. He turned around to look up at her, and he looked younger, almost like a child, twisted up like that.

"Call me?"

"She wanted to stay in touch with you about the donor." He sighed, rolling back over, and closed his eyes.

Her hand had stopped, it held his hair up like a gear shift.

"Mm," she said.

"I told her I didn't think that she should."

"It might not be the best idea," Emily said.

"No," he said. "It might not be."

"Has she used the vials?" The words almost didn't come out. She didn't want to think it. Not that it would change the situation. Or maybe it would. Because maybe she was the lace on the table, and the baby was the table. Or maybe the lace was the sperm, and the table was his marriage? Or maybe they were the table, and Belle was the lace? It got confusing, trying to figure out how to see things.

"No," he said. "No, she hasn't done it."

He sat up and turned to her. She waited for him to clarify. He reached out to touch her lips, but when he kissed her, he felt separate, just another person pressed to her.

"She still wants me to come around," he said.

"What are you going to do?" Emily asked.

"What do you mean?" he said.

"Are you going to come around?"

"To having a baby with her?"

"To that. I don't know. To Belle," Emily said.

He closed his eyes, but she could still see the movement of it beneath the lid. She had the briefest bodily memory of being at the very top of a sand-dune as a child with the wind whipping the grains into her skin, stinging her, and her mother nowhere in sight.

"I've been trying to figure out how to leave," he said. "I'd like to leave. I would. I just don't want to leave Cheryl," he said. They had named the baby Cheryl—or Belle had named it. Cheryl! Who names a baby Cheryl?

"You could move in with me," she said. "I'd take you."

Elliot turned toward the baby in her belly and pressed his nose to it. She wove her fingers in his hair. She imagined what the baby might say if it could speak through the placenta, uterus, muscle, and skin. The baby's words would be stay, stay, stay. Every baby's word would be stay.

Did it make her a terrible person? Elliot left. Emily stood with the dishes in the sink and let her hands dangle into the sudsy water. She could see a faint reflection of herself in the window that looked out to the courtyard of her building. It looked wet, the grass bent from the weather, the leaves in old decaying piles, the naked arms of a tree reaching up. It was so hard to explain it—and no matter how she tried, she couldn't erase Belle and Cheryl, the other two, the collateral damage. It was them or her. It couldn't be both. And so, of course, it should be her. Because he loved Emily, and he didn't love Belle and in the end it would be better for everyone. The cosmic math would come out the same. One baby would have a father and one would not. She couldn't adjust that. It fell outside of her powers. The world remained unfair but love made you honest. What more could anyone say about it?

"Is he going to marry you, then?" Mariette usually didn't ask questions like this. In the last few weeks she'd gone from a starved, black-clad style with lots of angles and leather, to a soft, bohemian look. Today she wore a large tunic with batik designs down the front in indigos and rusts. Her tight jeans had worn spots, frayed holes bitten in by some machine in China. Her toenails shone, a tangerine shellac. Mariette had lax rules for living. Rent a space, spend a little more than you made, whatever, it would all sort itself out in the end. But about Elliot she had been quiet.

"I don't know," Emily said.

"Is he going to stick around when you get bigger? Is he prepared for it all?

I mean, he must get it. He has one at home. Pretty soon it'll be hard for you to get around, to just take off your clothes and engage, so to speak. You're going to need someone solid, someone you can depend on. Then there's all the milk and spit up and shit, the screaming in the middle of the night. Your whole life will start to smell intimate, like you haven't showered, like you can't even remember a shower. Your house will start to have that infant smell, the least erotic smell in the world. Testosterone killer. I always thought making love with an infant in the room would feel like raping a kitten. Some women can do it, but I found it—well, revolting."

"Why are you saying this stuff to me?" Emily felt the mice with their frozen feet. Their feet bursting now into fire as they reached the base of her skull.

"I don't know," Mariette said. She slammed a picture down on the coffee table.

"I have to go," Emily said. She waited for Mariette to apologize. Who was she to pass judgment? Poni's father lived in some glass house in Beverley Hills with a young starlet wife and two small children. Mariette got cash from him in manila envelopes. Thousands of dollars, untraceable. Emily had seen the piles of it in the dinette area.

But Mariette didn't apologize. And that evening Elliot didn't text or call. Emily tried watching a show on the laptop. She played a video game on her phone. She felt listless and alone. She called a few friends from college that she still kept in touch with. Another who worked at a small press downtown. No one answered. She read about what was happening inside her. Nineteen weeks and her baby had started to turn from soft cartilage to bone, hardening into something breakable.

He said, the day before, that he might stop by but late. She had hours to wait and no food in the apartment. She had to go out.

The night felt cool but not unmanageably cold, and Emily's legs ached from sitting. She walked down the small neighborhood streets with their tall trees and old Craftsman houses. She loved these streets, the fantasy they represented. Everyone tucked inside their homes, warm and dry, pantries of soup, of beans and dried fruit, little children in footy pajamas calling out for bedtime stories, a cat in a window grooming a leg. Lives of hard work and ethical grocery shopping and hybrid cars. Two months ago, newly pregnant, this tableau had alienated her, made her upset, made her feel like she'd been forever sealed out of a fate she yearned for. The whole world seemed in on it. But now she felt differently. She felt like she might be able to walk up to a door and simply open it, enter one of those grand foyers, lightly sprint up the carpeted steps to a master bedroom with oil paintings on the wall, with homemade curtains, and fling herself onto clean down blankets. Elliot, Elliot, Elliot—it was making her dizzy and dumb, or maybe the hormones were. She felt like a girl with a Sharpie and a three-ring-binder, writing Elliot in cursive, doodling a house and a flower and a dog and a smiling sun.

At first, the woman in the booth at the Thai place on Belmont only looked familiar in a vague way, like a dental hygienist or a nurse. Someone she briefly dealt with. Long blond hair and bright blue eyes, crazy eyes, with spikey lashes. A peach-colored peasant blouse and big silver jewelry. But then her face clicked into its correct location in Emily's mind. Belle. She sat alone, though it appeared someone just left the table. The chair across from hers sat akimbo. A bottle of Ninkasi lager, a pot sticker cooling on a plate.

She had time. She could just back out of the door the same way she came in. She jerked her arm off the hostess counter, and a small plastic toothpick dispenser came smacking to the ground.

Belle looked over and her face went from blank to scrunched to smiling. She waved rapidly at Emily. Emily pretended not to see, pretended to study the way the toothpick contraption had landed. She picked it up, carefully set it back in its place. Shit Shit. Shit.

"I was thinking about calling you!" Belle said. "But I've been so busy with house repairs. Do you want to sit with us? You don't need to eat alone."

Elliot emerged from the bathroom in the back. He stood still, watching them.

"Oh no, no, I'm fine, really, I was only getting takeout, thanks."

"Well, just come say hi," Belle said. She smelled strongly of drugstore lotion, or maybe that was the pregnancy smelling things. Emily could smell every fruit shampoo, every lotion and deodorant brand these days.

Elliot returned to his seat, his face inscrutable and pale. He took his baseball hat off and ran a hand through his hair. She wanted to smile, to do their melting eyes, to put her hand on his hair, too, and run it the wrong way so she could feel each piece of it against her skin. "Let's get out of here," she'd say. She could turn to Belle and tell her: "He's been unhappy. So unhappy. You wouldn't want that in your life. You can't raise a happy child in such unhappiness." They could drive back to San Francisco, rent another small place in the Mission—or if the tech companies had driven prices too high, Oakland, Emeryville, Vallejo, it didn't matter. They could live on burritos and raise this baby and make films and on weekends go sit on the beach, the city lights streaking over the hills, the bridges arching over the Bay. People did crazier things! They could eat dumplings and oysters and teach the baby how to recite a poem, how to make a castle. But those were just the small things. They'd actually teach something far more delicate and insistent, far more crucial. They would teach the baby how to risk, how to live with her skin right up against bone, how to make the world happen for her. They would teach the baby how to love.

She walked over to the table and stood dumbly over it.

"Sweetie," said Belle, "do you remember Emily? With the extra vials?"

He nodded and his eyes turned playful, that familiar swimmy spark, and Emily almost did it, almost threw herself down in front of him and made her speech, but then his face closed up and a flicker of something much darker played across his eyes. Was it shame? And he said, "Oh, right, hi." And Belle started talking about something, about how wonderful it felt to see her there, but Emily couldn't hear her, only the tinny sound of something being emitted, something problematic and close, but not meant for her.

"You must be pretty much over the worst of the pregnancy by now, right? I mean, it gets uglier looking, but not uglier feeling, really, till the bitter end." Belle put a hand on Emily's belly. Emily stopped breathing. She felt the warmth through her shirt, through her skin.

"Do you want a pot sticker?" Elliot said. No one responded. The pot

sticker looked glued to the plate, the fake grass decoration beneath it imper-
tinently green, cockeyed, jaunty.

"We had a late night with Cheryl," Belle finally said. "Everyone's a little
tired. We're so grateful for our date nights. They're so rare." Belle reached her
hand out to Elliot. He sat with his hands in his lap and didn't reach back.
Emily watched Belle's hand there, untouched—like watching a car drive
slowly into a wall. Belle reached a little further toward him, bending slightly
at the hips. Then finally, Elliot darted his hand out to touch Belle's, and then
withdrew it into his lap again.

Emily felt a burning in her esophagus.

"Well, we're just out enjoying our relative freedom because we have a big
day at the doctor's tomorrow," Belle said, winking.

Unbidden, an image of Belle naked on a cushioned table at the doctor's
with her legs spread wide in front of Elliot. Gray labia opening to pink raw
flesh. A doctor with sterile tubing, inserting it up Belle's vaginal passageway
toward her tender cervix. The image brought with it a too-human smell, raw
and iron-like. And that did it. It gave her no warning, just rammed open her
jaw and sent white fluid across the table, right onto Belle's peach peasant
blouse and over her silver bangles.

Elliot didn't call or text. He didn't the next night either. A darkness grew in
the apartment. The baby grew. And it seemed like overnight she grew, too.
Her breasts expanded, sunk down a little, her hips drew outward, toward
the walls of the house. None of her pants fit except the elastic ones. Her hair
went lank, dark welts beneath her eyes. She wanted to text him and say I am
so sorry, I am so embarrassed, but she was too sorry and too embarrassed.

She looked at herself naked in the standing mirror. She recognized herself and didn't recognize herself. The skin on her body became a costume
she wore. She impersonated a pregnant woman. She did a very good job at
it.

She cleaned the apartment, tossing old spices, stray socks. She washed
her dishes in hot water, mopped the floor. Mariette finally called her and
invited her over for breakfast. Her college friends called her back, one after

the other. She felt something happening inside of her, something blooming wet and vivid, of her and not of her, like a yolk.

He finally called. She sat in the small shared editing studio, which lately had no other tenants. She worked on a local ad campaign, smoothing out the footage, cutting and splicing until it played seamlessly. She stared at the flashing name: Elliot and then she clawed at her phone.

"Elliot," she said.

"Hi, Emily. He spoke her name with a downward cadence, the last syllable underground and muted. Her heart sank.

"I'm so sorry," she said.

"Don't be sorry," he said. "Really, I'm the one that should be sorry."

"No," she said.

"I'm sorry," he said. "You know why I'm calling."

She sat there, turning to stone—or not turning to stone. If only she could turn to stone, but she could not. She would not. She would go on being very much alive.

"Emily?" he said. "I can't talk long. I have to go to work. But I couldn't leave you waiting anymore. I know you'll hate me. I know. I hate me, too."

He had to go to work. What was he doing? Showing a house? Meeting with clients? Helping someone spruce up a bungalow, paint over the places where leaks stained the wall?

"I think you're so wonderful," he said. "I know you'll find someone more deserving of you."

She pressed the little button on her phone and watched his name disappear.

Elliot and Belle. The unhappy familiar had its own seductions.

She sat for a while, until something red and ugly began to happen inside of her. She wanted to call back: How could you do this to me! How could you walk away from me, from us! She felt like throwing herself to the floor and tearing at her hair. She would be alone—maybe forever. Who would love her now? What had she done to herself? How had she so irrevocably messed up her life? And how could she tolerate it? But the baby chose that moment to move.

Hey, the baby said with a fluttering movement—different from others she'd felt. It's me.

She hadn't meant to be brave. She hadn't meant to be fearless. She'd meant, only, to be Emily. She hadn't intended to live this way, but life kept on arriving, disheveled and stupidly honest.

The baby moved again, this time unmistakably.

She set her hand there, where the baby had kicked, where she'd been kicked, where a flutter met skin, where something she didn't yet know made contact with what she did.

ACKNOWLEDGMENTS

Thank you to these wonderful magazines, where my stories first appeared: *Sewanee Review, Zyzzyva, The Missouri Review, The Antioch Review*, and *Shenandoah*. Thanks also to the O'Henry Prize committee for the meaningful honor bestowed on *Marital Problems*, and to the Lannan Foundation and The MacDowell Colony where, before children, I worked on these stories. Thank you to the incredible teachers who've cared for, taught, and loved our kids while I have worked, particularly Laura and Gaea at Giving Tree. Thanks to Martha Rhodes and Ryan Murphy at Four Way Books for seeing something special in this project. Thanks to my father, Richard, for many layers of support. And thank you to the best people ever, Don, Sylvie, and Annie, for deepening my humanity, bestowing me with perspective, and remaking me for the better. You are everywhere, obviously, in this book.

ABOUT THE AUTHOR

Robin Romm is the author of two short story collections, *The Mother Garden*, and *Radical Empathy*; a chapbook of stories, *The Tilt*; as well as a memoir, *The Mercy Papers* (a New York Times Notable Book). She also compiled and edited the essay collection, *Double Bind: Women on Ambition*. She's been awarded an O'Henry Prize in short fiction, and was a finalist for the Pen USA prize for her first collection. Her journalism and nonfiction writing have appeared in *The Atlantic*, *The New York Times*, *Wired*, *O Magazine*, *Parents*, and *Slate*. She lives in Portland, Oregon, with her partner, the writer Don Waters, and their two spitfire daughters.

PUBLICATION OF THIS BOOK WAS MADE POSSIBLE
BY GRANTS AND DONATIONS. WE ARE ALSO GRATEFUL
TO THOSE INDIVIDUALS WHO PARTICIPATED IN
OUR BUILD A BOOK PROGRAM. THEY ARE:

Anonymous (14), Robert Abrams, Debra Allbery, Nancy Allen, Michael
Ansara, Kathy Aponick, Jean Ball, Sally Ball, Jill Bialosky, Sophie Cabot
Black, Laurel Blossom, Tommye Blount, Karen and David Blumenthal,
Jonathan Blunk, Lee Briccetti, Jane Martha Brox, Mary Lou Buschi,
Anthony Cappo, Carla and Steven Carlson, Robin Rosen Chang, Liza
Charlesworth, Peter Coyote, Elinor Cramer, Kwame Dawes, Michael Anna
de Armas, Brian Komei Dempster, Renko and Stuart Dempster, Matthew
DeNichilo, Rosalynde Vas Dias, Patrick Donnelly, Charles R. Douthat,
Lynn Emanuel, Blas Falconer, Laura Fjeld, Carolyn Forché, Helen Fremont
and Donna Thagard, Debra Gitterman, Dorothy Tapper Goldman,
Alison Granucci, Elizabeth T. Gray, Jr., Naomi Guttman and Jonathan
Meade, Jeffrey Harrison, KT Herr, Carlie Hoffman, Melissa Hotchkiss,
Thomas and Autumn Howard, Catherine Hoyser, Elizabeth Jackson,
Linda Susan Jackson, Jessica Jacobs, Deborah Jonas-Walsh, Jennifer Just,
Voki Kalfayan, Maeve Kinkead, Victoria Korth, David Lee and Jamila
Trindle, Rodney Terich Leonard, Howard Levy, Owen Lewis and Susan
Ennis, Eve Linn, Matthew Lippman, Ralph and Mary Ann Lowen, Maja
Lukic, Neal Lulofs, Anthony Lyons, Ricardo Alberto Maldonado, Trish
Marshall, Donna Masini, Deborah McAlister, Carol Moldaw, Michael and
Nancy Murphy, Kimberly Nunes, Matthew Olzmann and Vivee Francis,
Veronica Patterson, Patrick Phillips, Robert Pinsky, Megan Pinto, Kevin
Prufer, Anna Duke Reach, Paula Rhodes, Loki Robusto, Yoana Setzer,
James Shalek, Soraya Shalforoosh, Peggy Shinner, Joan Silber, Jane Simon,
Debra Spark, Donna Spruijt-Metz, Arlene Stang, Page Hill Starzinger,
Catherine Stearns, Yerra Sugarman, Laurence Tancredi, Marjorie and Lew
Tesser, Peter Turchi, Connie Voisine, Susan Walton, Martha Webster
and Robert Fuentes, Calvin Wei, Allison Benis White, Lauren Yaffe, Rolf
Yngve, and Arthur Sze.